Rumor &

Deception

THE HIGHLY ANTICIPATED SEQUEL TO
"RUMOR: DAUGHTER OF LIES"

"NEVER TRUST PERFECTION,
FOR IT IS ONLY A BEAUTIFULLY DECORATED FORM OF
DECEPTION."

From the mind of

J.E. Tyler

ISBN-13: 978-0692454589
ISBN-10: 0692454586

DEDICATION

There is not one life in this world that is not worthy of the divine image in which it was created. We are all God's children, and I'd like to dedicate this novel to the movement for American justice and equality. All lives matter. #BlackLivesMatter

ACKNOWLEDGEMENTS

It takes a full lifetime for some people to realize the destiny that God has placed on their lives. I'm forever grateful to my Father in heaven for the opportunity to be walking within my destiny. I want to give a special thanks to both my parents, James and Cassandra Tyler, who have encouraged me every step of the way.

I also want to thank everyone who has contributed to the masterpiece which is in your hands: Nakira McCrea, Nathan "AdmirerGq" Manneh, Kelvin Bulluck at KelB Pics Photography, Nye' Lyn Tho Designs, and Lyn at Strategic Solutions.

To anyone who has supported my gift by reading any of my published words, I cannot thank you enough. This journey has been a blessing for me. I promise that if you all continue to support me, this journey will be a true blessing for us all.

Continue to tell all of your friends, family and loved ones about these amazing novels. Let's discuss Rumor on all Social Media with the hashtag #SpreadTheRumor. I look forward to hearing from you soon.

Contents

CHAPTER 1

A Tainted Shield

As Told By D

I wasn't just your average black market goon; I was respected as a boss, because I was the number one hustler on the streets. No one could match my skills for manipulating the minds and emotions of the every-day man. That is why the most powerful and influential men of New Orleans trusted me to do their dirty work.

Confidently I walked through the dark and secret locations where the righteous men of the city came to plot their true malicious intentions. City councilman, district attorneys, judges, senators, and all kinds of high ranking officials traded, sold, bought, and profited off the pain and misery of the destitute citizens of the city. You'd be surprised at how many suits lay down big bills for a peek at some live child pornography. Human trafficking was just as common as stocks on Wall Street. My personal favorite, blood diamonds, seemed to attract only the fattest pockets.

On that particular night, I wasn't there for leisure; I was walking through the halls of underground criminal markets as a man on a mission for business. We were in the basement of a downtown hotel; it was one of the many random locations where the market was held. At the end of a long, obscure hallway, I stopped at a room where I was given orders to knock to the beat of the first line of Twinkle Little Star. The direction didn't even surprise me. The kind of discrete criminals who frequented the black markets were often paranoid to the point of insanity.

As soon as the door opened, a large fist came lunging in my direction. My instincts were keen and my reflexes were quick. I stepped out of the trajectory of the plunging knuckles, grabbed the man's arm, and used his own momentum to fling him into the wall behind me. That's when he drew two knives from the sleeves of his suit jacket. I stood calmly as he swung ferociously in my direction. I blocked each swing with my forearms before unleashing a swift high kick directly into his chin. His neck nearly snapped as his body jolted backwards to the floor.

"You are a very impressive man. I hope you're not upset by my welcoming committee Mr. Ception. I've heard so many stories about your skills. I just had to witness it for myself." A man spoke from behind the anonymity of a large, leather office chair. He never once turned so that I could see his face. I assumed that hiding behind the chair was one of his tactics for discretion. He spoke with a very energetic and charismatic tone. Each sentence contained the expert timing of a stand-up comedian.

"I like this one, Big Daddy. Can we bring him home?" a very busty bright-skinned woman with curves, that could only be concocted on top of some operating table, giggled like a little school girl.

"Not this time, baby. This is business. Maybe when our plans are complete, Mr. Ception will join us for a little ménage á trios." said the mystery man.

"Sorry, but I have strict rules against fraternizing with clientele. Tell me about the job." I said while quickly growing tired of the man's antics.

"Of course. As you know, I'm the one who gave you the envelope with the paperwork for your latest identity. I need an inside man with the N.O.P.D."

"Yeah, I figured that. What do you need from me?"

"Police Chief Troy is wiping out the local gangs with his community service initiatives and that's not good for business. I have an entire armory of military ammunition that cost me a lot of money. If I don't sell it, I take a huge loss. I don't take losses, so I need those gangs up and operating."

"So you want me to sabotage Chief Troy's initiatives?" I said trying to understand the end game.

"No, let the Chief have his fun. We're about to start a street war of cops versus thugs, and that's where I need your help Mr. Ception." As he spoke, I could hear him grinning through his tone. He followed with a creepy laugh that sounded like the struggling gasps of a dying man.

"As I'm sure you know, my services don't come cheap, especially for a job as risky as this one sounds." I could see my business card sitting on his desk. It was a black card with the name D. Ception in red letters; there was no other information besides my name. That card was my only method for promoting my services in the streets. All of the other information came on a need-to-know basis and my reputation usually delivered it.

"Finish this job and there will be fifty million dollars in unmarked bills waiting for you." His words were like music to my ears. The man was clearly a psychopath, but I was growing tired of the life of a hustler. This job would be my way out of the hellacious underground life that I had created for myself.

As I turned to step over my injured attacker and proceed down the long, murky hallway, I looked into a mirror on the wall. My hustles were beginning to consume me. Half the time, I didn't even recognize myself. No one knew that I was really only 18-years-old. A rough life on the streets left me with the appearance of a man in his late 20s, but inside, I felt much older. For this particular job, I would be 23- year-old cop, Darryl Walker.

It's always been so funny to me how most of these cats put on a blue uniform, a holster, and a corny badge, and actually believe that they have some kind of real power. These fools are just a bunch of jokes. The real bad boys are on the streets, hiding behind the disguise of normalcy. Real recognizes real, so I could see it in their eyes; the urge for violence and the unquenchable thirst for chaos were all too real.

Street thugs were in the midst of picket signs and sweet old ladies who cried for change, but I can guarantee you that half of them didn't even know what they were protesting for. They couldn't even tell you the full name of the 10-year-old unarmed black kid who was gunned down by a trigger-happy rookie cop last month. That boy couldn't be further from their minds right now. They sensed chaos on the rise, so now their purpose was to ensure its existence. Now to those who wonder why someone on the right side of the barricade, like me, would identify more with the criminals than his fellow cops; not every officer's shield is made of real steel. Some of us were forged by deception.

"I hope you found your balls, Mack. The streets are about to get live." I could barely hear myself speaking over the protestor's shouting. We were only minutes away from the jury's decision and the crowd was growing more uneasy with each second.

"Don't play me, D. I've seen worse than this." Officer Ron Mack tried his hardest to hide the nerve quaking anxiety that was building within him.

"Oh yea? Did somebody tip over the ice cream truck back in Nowhere, Mississippi?" I smirked. I enjoyed getting under Mack's skin. The dude was so damn good and decent that it made me sick. I was tired of him pissing on my mornings with talks of police reports and unclosed cases.

"Real funny. How about you keep your eye on that crowd, and let me worry about me?" said Mack.

"If anything, they'd better keep their eyes on me." I said while clinching the handle of the glock that rested in my holster.

The afternoon sun was setting on New Orleans' horizon. I'd spent six months in the academy, and one year on the streets pretending to be dedicated to justice, all in preparation for this moment. War was within our reach and my pockets were about to be good and fat because of it.

As the thought of riches graced my mind, the low, smooth blowing of a jazz hymn sounded from several large trumpets. The protestors all cleared a path as a small jazz band ushered the dead kid's family towards the center of the crowd. I had to give it to New Orleans, even in the midst of tragedy, there was a marching band.

Just when I felt the marching spectacle could not be any more ridiculous, what appeared to be the Great Christmas Tree came sashaying among their ranks. She wore a green, flowing gown with a white feather boa draped across her neck. A bob-styled beach blonde hairdo framed her chunky, almond brown face. She had to be no shorter than 6'3", as she towered over the men in the band. I swear her backside was as wide as the bumper on a Buick truck. She was as large and intimidating as your average night club bouncer, but she easily moved with the grace and eloquence of a pageant queen. As the family of the slain young man took their seats on a raised platform, the oversized black Barbie doll faced the crowd with a microphone in hand.

"Ahem." As she cleared her throat for attention, a deep, raspy baritone voice echoed throughout the packed streets. I was stunned. I couldn't believe what I was hearing. She sounded like a chain-smoking, 50-year-old man.

"Mack, go get your girlfriend off the mic before she can embarrass herself anymore," I said, finding humor in Ron Mack's disgust as the large woman pulled at the underwear beneath her gown in an attempt to adjust her stance.

"Shut the hell up!" Mack barked in retaliation.

"I said, ahem." The woman retorted while directing her

attention towards a couple of front row protestors locked in a private conversation. "As many of you know, I'm Neffie Lestránge. I own Lestránge's Tavern over yonder about three blocks down. Yea, that's mine, and I better not catch any of you lootin' assholes on my premises. Ya' hear me?"

"Neffie!" A man shouted from behind her.

"Fine!" Neffie yelled. "But that's not why I'm here today. In honor of my best girlfriend's son, Nicholas Macon, I want to sing a little something special."

The thought of her rugged voice singing through blasting speakers left my nerves on edge. Police Chief Troy paced back and forth. I could tell he was anxious for the court room decision to end the display of foolishness occurring on the platform.

Surprisingly, a wave of immense vocal talent filled the streets. I couldn't imagine that it was coming from Neffie, but her voice rivaled Aretha Franklin's during her days of youth and glory. It was unbelievable. She sang Hezekiah Walker's song "I'll Fly Away." Each note she sang tugged at the emotions of the crowd. From some of them she elicited great sorrow and tears, but amongst those with criminal intention, she only fueled their anger; they were primed and ready to unleash destruction. The jury's verdict would be the final recipe to that afternoon's concoction of chaos. I was growing impatient. I needed action. I couldn't imagine what was taking the jury so long.

"Thank you, Neffie." said Lawanda Macon, the mother of the deceased young man as she finally stood to face the crowd. Her eyes were heavy and wet with tears. She seemed thin and drained from her days of grieving. Anyone with a heart could not help but be emotionally touched by her somber sight, but I had no heart. What little heart I had left was destroyed long ago by the reality that I had been condemned too. My mother had never cried for me, so I couldn't possibly find a way to relate to Lawanda's loss.

"There's not a night that goes by in which I don't think about my baby boy. He was so full of life. He would run around the streets with his friends all day. All the kids in the neighborhood loved him. Your kids loved him. I can look out at some of you today and see them in your faces. They'd come knocking on my door begging for Nick to come out and play. I'd smile and yell for Nicholas to come down," Lawanda painfully described her son to an audience of mourners that knew him personally. "Watching my little boy run out into the yard, I never thought the day would come where he wouldn't come running back. I let my baby leave to enjoy a neighborhood that I pay taxes for; we pay taxes for this city. This is our home, and how dare they kill our children? Our children. I can see your children's faces in all of you. They loved Nick and my baby's gone. He can no longer go out to play because his life was taken by the same men who swore to protect him every single day. My baby is gone, and still your children cry out for him through your faces. Nick can't come out to play, but you can help me ensure justice for my baby today. Justice for Nick!" Lawanda's voice trembled as she struggled to hold back tears.

"Justice for Nick!" the protestors shouted in unison.

An onrush of energy erupted throughout the streets. Picket signs, clinched fists, and cries for justice rose into the air. Chief Troy ordered us all to hold our ranks as the protestors' activities escalated. I attempted to hide the pleasure on my face as the bad boys of the crowd stepped to the front lines of the protest. I was now facing them. They were my kindred spirits.

"People of New Orleans, please believe that we are all touched by Ms. Macon's grief, but I need you all to remain peaceful in your assembly," Chief Troy shouted with the aid of a bull horn.

"No justice, no peace!" one voice shouted in protest before all of the other's joined in with the chant.

"If you do not comply, we will be forced to unleash the tear gas," Chief Troy warned.

"New Orleans, I am begging you to please remain peaceful. For Nick, we must do this the right way. Please do not tarnish my child's legacy with violence." Lawanda's voice rang from the speakers as she pleaded for peace.

Even with Lawanda's emotional influence, she was no match for the rage that had built within the crowd. We raised our shields in preparation to rush them all. Even without the jury's decision, war was inevitable.

Without warning, a glass bottle soared from amongst the protestors and crashed at our feet. The chief ordered us to wear our masks as we filled the sky with clouds of tear gas. I was filled with exhilaration as my police shield collided with the skulls of the innocent. The base of my Billy club was stained with blood as I viciously attacked every civilian in sight. I was at my best. I was savage. I had completely lost my mind to the animal that I truly am.

"Darryl, fall back!" Ron Mack grabbed me, pulling me away from the protestors.

"Get off me!" I snapped before swinging my Billy club into Mack's face.

"What the hell are you doing?" Mack shouted as I attempted to pummel him with my club.

"Get off me!" I continued to yell as other officers pulled me away.

"It's over, fool. The jury didn't reach a decision. It's over," Mack yelled.

It was over. The jury had failed to reach a decision. My war had been halted, and my beast was exposed. I was furious.

I later inhaled deeply, bringing in the steam-filled, musty air of the precinct locker room. I sat contemplating on that day's failure as hot shower water ran over my tired body. I took a look down at my callas-ridden hands and shuttered at the thought of damage they caused. I made a living off of damaging the lives of others and I didn't feel a single bit of remorse. Mentally I found myself in a very peculiar place. It was one of the rare moments in which I wished that I could feel positive emotions like normal people. I wanted to be human, but even with gallons of hot water flowing over my naked body; I could still feel the lingering filth of my past. I was a lost cause.

The steel walls of my locker vibrated and hummed beneath the ringing of my cell phone. I grabbed a fresh towel and wrapped it around my waist. The screen on my phone read, Kesha. I wasn't in the mood for Kesha's crazy talk, but with my main hustle on hold, I needed Kesha's inheritance to keep me going.

I answered the phone, "Hello."

"Darryl, where the hell have you been? I've been calling you all day." Kesha's tongue-popping ghetto accent made it hard to believe that she was worth millions. Her father was literally the Mardi Gras king. He owned the best Mardi Gras museums, ballrooms, and festivals in the city, and his only child was my spoiled little cash cow.

"Kesha, I told you I can't always answer the phone during the day. I'm a cop dammit!"

"My period is on. I've got cramps. I need you to rub my feet baby." Kesha whimpered like a 3-year-old. I didn't know how long I would be able to maintain my hustle over Kesha. She was annoying the hell out of me.

"I'll be home in an hour," I said before ending the call.

No sooner than the light of my phone had gone dim, I looked up to see Ron Mack standing before me. His eye was dark and swollen to the size of a burnt biscuit. Chief Troy was so furious that he couldn't even look me in the eye as he told me I was suspended indefinitely without pay. I really messed up, but I was still in the game and Ron Mack was about to be my next pawn.

"I got you pretty good, huh?" I chuckled to make light of the situation.

"Man, what the hell is wrong with you? Why do you hate me so much?" Mack fumed.

"Who said anything about hating you?" I asked.

"I don't know, maybe it was the Billy club that bashed my damn eye!" Mack snapped.

"I don't know what to tell you, Mack. I blacked out. I may have hit you, but I wasn't seeing you," I said.

"You should really talk to someone, man. Get some help. You're a pretty good cop and my first partner with the NOPD. Maybe it's the small town mentality, but I was hoping we'd end up best friends or something."

"I ain't never had a friend, man. This is a dog-eat-dog world. Nobody gives a damn about me or what I'm going through. Why the hell should I talk? Nobody's listening."

"You don't get it do you, man? I'm sitting here with a black eye that you gave me, and my ears are still open. I've seen some messed up stuff where I come from bro. There ain't much you can tell me that I won't believe." said Mack.

"C'mon man, you're the son of a small town sheriff, born and raised in one of those places where everybody knows your name. You can't relate to the life I've lived."

"Try me." Ron sat down on the bench beside me. I couldn't take that dude seriously. I damn near dug his eye out of its socket with my baton, and there he was trying to help me. If I didn't need an ear on the inside of the justice system, I would've finished pummeling his jacked up eye.

"Ok, you wanna stroll down the yellow brick road with the Tin Man? Well here it is. I was raised by a teenage crack feign. It was just me and her. Since she was coked out of her mind half the time, I pretty much raised myself. I learned from the streets. I became the streets. All I knew was survival, man, and that doesn't include family or friendships," I explained.

"So you mean to tell me no one ever cared? No one ever showed you any kind of love?" asked Ron. I could tell by the way that his eyes tightened that his mind was busy trying to figure me out.

"There was this one woman about ten years ago. I was just a skinny kid, pick-pocketing assholes on the street for change. That's when I saw her. She was beautiful, man, with a long pair of legs that just wouldn't quit and the sweetest face that I've ever seen on a woman. I couldn't believe a woman that beautiful was selling ass on the streets. With a face and body like that, she could've had any man she wanted." As I spoke, I could see it all transpiring in my mind as if it had just happened the day before.

"So what happened?" Ron urged me to continue.

"I picked the wrong damn pocket, bruh. All I know is four rock hard knuckles slammed across my little face. I dropped like a bag of bricks. I really thought dude was going to kill me. Sometimes I wish he had. It just wasn't my time yet because God sent the most beautiful angel to help me out. She jumped between us and begged him to stop hitting me. It turned out dude was her pimp."

"So he let you go?" asked Mack.

"Yeah, he let me go. She took me to a diner across the street and bought me a hot meal to eat while she finished her shift on the corner. Man, the way she looked at me, I could tell that she wasn't really seeing me; she was seeing someone else. It had to be someone she really loved and missed a lot. I know I would've killed to have my mother show me even half the love that was in that woman's eyes. I wanted to know more about her, but I never got the chance."

"Why not?"

"Before she could even finish her shift, that damn pimp had

his hands around her neck. I could tell by the way she was gagging that he was killing her. She was the only person who'd ever shown me any kind of love man. Even if that love was for someone else, it felt real good to be on the receiving end of it. I couldn't just let that go."

"So what did you do?"

"I killed the fool. I stole a used steak knife from one of the tables at the diner. He didn't even see me coming. The streets had trained me well. That blade cut through his flesh so easily. It felt good to have his life in my hands. I felt more important than I'd ever felt in my life. I wasn't just some poor street rat. I was a taker of life. I felt like a god."

I could tell that I said too much by the look of concern on Ron Mack's face. He was a small town boy who thought he'd seen it all until he met a natural born killer. It was so typical. Everybody claimed to want the truth, but none of them could ever handle it. His expression was only confirmation for my fraudulent lifestyle.

"You killed him?" Mack stammered over his words.

"I did, but his death came at a price. She saw the satisfaction in my eyes. She saw the animal in me, and in that moment, she couldn't see the person she missed any longer. She couldn't see her loved one, most likely her child. When she was really able to see the true me, she feared me. She screamed for help. I couldn't get her to calm down. She just kept screaming. The cops came and I ended up spending the next four years in juvie."

"Man, that's crazy."

"Tell me about it. I'm not that animal anymore though man. I lost that part of me in juvie," I lied.

"I understand. I'm not here to judge you, man. My hometown wasn't exactly a bed of roses for the sheriff's oldest son either. I didn't come to New Orleans for ambition man. I came here running away from my own shame," Ron admitted.

"Shame? What kind of shame could a boy scout like you possibly have?"

"I knocked up my little brother's teenage girlfriend. It was bad, man. It was real bad, but what made it even worse is the fact that I loved her. I still love her. I had to leave, because if I had stayed, there's no way I would've been able to resist her." Mack pulled his wallet from his back pocket and opened it to reveal a small picture.

"This her?" I said while eyeing the picture. She was a beauty, but the younger girl who stood next to her caught my eye. Looking at her was like looking directly into my past. She had the exact same face as my angel. The resemblance was uncanny.

"Yeah that picture is old, but that's Gia. She's the only girl I've ever loved. The other girl is her little cousin, Rumor." Answered Rumor. I repeated the name Rumor as the image of the girl glued itself to my mind.

I couldn't erase Rumor from my thoughts. Later that evening, I sat in Kesha's apartment googling Rumor Arden. She was 15-years-old at the time. It turned out there was a high profile story behind the face of the small town angel. She was the grand-daughter of the legendary crime-boss Vendetta Gatto. V. Gatto was a legend on the southern streets. The woman had secured so many avenues of loot that not even the FBI could touch it all. As Gatto's only surviving next of kin, Rumor was only a few years shy of being a wealthy, southern princess. I was intrigued.

"Damn, Darryl, are you gon' rub my feet or not? I ain't seen you all day and you ain't touched me once since you walked through that door." Kesha nagged relentlessly.

"My bad babe. Pull out the KY. I'm about to massage a lot more than them feet." I turned around and gave her a wink that sent chills through her body. She turned and ran into the bedroom, where I soon followed her.

Kesha was wild in the bedroom, and pleasing her cakes left me more than a little exhausted. I slept hard that night, but I dreamed even harder. Rumor's beautiful face glimmered before me like the North Star. I couldn't help but caress the smooth, brown skin of her face. I wanted to kiss her so badly, but as my lips approached hers, my dream faded into fury and unimaginable heat.

"Who the hell is Rumor?" Kesha doused scowling hot water across my neck and chest. I rolled over onto the floor cringing with excruciating pain.

"Are you trying to kill me?" I yelled.

"Answer the question, nigga!" Kesha screamed. "You are sleeping in my damn bed, dream-talking about some chick that you've been googling on my computer. You done lost your damn mind!"

"Kesha, you need to chill!" I shouted.

"Who are you talking to? You need to answer my damn question. That's what you need to do." Kesha continued to roll her neck and eyes while pushing against my forehead with her pointer finger.

"Kesha, I'm warning you." I could feel myself losing control. She was pushing the wrong buttons. The last thing I wanted to do was harm Kesha. She was my current source of income, but with every demeaning word she spoke, I could hear my mother's voice. I could feel my mother's rejection, and the hatred of an abandoned child was just too much for me to control.

"My Daddy was right about you niggas. You sit up and use me for my damn money while sticking your meat inside some other chick. Who is Rumor?"

"Shut the hell up!" I exploded, and before I knew it, I had slapped Kesha with the full extent of my strength. She fell and hit her temporal lobe on the sharp corner of her nightstand.

"Kesha," I bawled as her body erupted into convulsions. She shook uncontrollably into several seizures before her eye's pupils disappeared completely. I held her tightly as she took her last breath. Kesha was dead.

I was off the force indefinitely and the jury's decision on the officer's guilt had not even been rescheduled. I had lost control of everything. In one day, I went from being an expert hustler to a serial screw up. I knew that if I didn't regain my edge soon, I could lose everything. It was only a matter of time before my client realized that I was no longer active on the force. I needed a plan B to hold me over until I could figure things out. With Kesha dead, I would no longer be able to use her father's money or influence. I needed a new hustle, and it turned out that her name was Rumor.

D's Journal Entry 1

I'm like a shadow under this tainted shield,
I got a glock 9 and its plated steel.
The barrel's aimed and the heat is real,
I keep it cocked, triggered and ready to kill.
It's just the beast in me that'll never yield,
My cards are cut and it's the devil's deal.
I've been lost my way and can't control my will,
So I'll rock this piece until my peace be still.

CHAPTER 2

The Never Loved
As Told By Rumor

When they're in the air, the clouds always seem so majestic. But on that particular evening, they were nothing more than a collection of fog hovering over the ground. Lying with my back against the mist filled grass and my eyes focused on the starry sky, I couldn't help but feel a sense of euphoria. Everything was so peaceful and serene, and with the clouds having descended onto the ground, the sky was clear and beautiful. In the three years following the chaotic events surrounding the death of my mother, I learned to appreciate the serenity of nature. I can't remember the last time I actually ran alongside the butterflies, because now I would just lie still and observe the patterns of their wings. It felt good to be able to embrace a moment with no interruptions; that is until the call of modern technology rang through like a giant bell.

"C'mon Taylor, you know the rules. No cell phones." I said while cutting my eyes toward Taylor with an annoyed expression.

"My bad, Rumor. It's Rima. She's been bad mouthing me on Facebook ever since we broke up." The light of Taylor's cell phone illuminated the amount of worry in his eyes. At 6' 2", Taylor was the only freshman boy on our high school's Varsity basketball team. During the last few months of our eighth grade year, Coach Khaled's car was always outside of Taylor's home. I'm sure Taylor's mother's flirtations played a small role in the coach's interest, but Taylor's height and athletic ability were definitely the driving force. They were driving forces so powerful that they'd catapulted my best friend to the highest levels of teenage popularity. All the boys wanted to be Taylor, and all the girls went into hormonal fits at the mention of his name. It was so weird witnessing Taylor's evolution first hand, because even with all the hoopla, all I could ever see was the shy, little boy who had always stuck to my side like glue.

"I told you Rima was crazy in the first place. I don't know why you keep entertaining these psycho chicks." I propped myself up by pushing my elbows against the ground to face Taylor's distraught face.

"She kept coming at me. What was I supposed to do? Rima's a bad chick. If I had turned her down, all the guys on the team would've clowned me," Taylor complained.

"Okay, so you chose to wife her instead, and now she's on the internet clowning you every day."

"Whatever, Rumor. You don't understand. I don't know why I even expected that you would get it." Taylor sighed.

"What's that supposed to mean?" I asked, taking offense to his insinuation that I couldn't understand his dilemma.

"Nothing. Don't worry about it." Taylor said.

"No, Taylor. Say what's on your mind. '*Poor, little unpopular Rumor, she can never get it. She's too much of an outcaste to understand normal teenagers.*' That's messed up Taylor," I said, wielding sarcasm like a sharp sword.

"Calm down. That's not even what I'm trying to say. I'm just saying..."

"Do tell. What exactly are you saying?" my voice was filled with attitude.

"I'm just saying you've never even had a boyfriend, Rumor. How could you understand? You don't know anything about love."

"Oh, really? And you do?" I shouted.

"Now you're getting in your feelings. You asked me a question, and I answered it. Chill out."

"You know what, Taylor. The only time I ever feel normal is when I'm with you. We were always on the same page until you got hit by a truck and grew 2 feet in 2 years."

"That's not cool. We've always been on the same page and we always will be." said Taylor.

"No, we're not. I'm still a little caterpillar dreaming of soaring with the butterflies. You, on the other hand, already have your wings, so why don't you just quit patronizing me and fly away like everyone else." As the words left my mouth, the emotions behind them were overwhelming. The sting of being left behind by my best friend was too much for me to bear. I tried to avoid it, but the truth was as unavoidable as Taylor's height. His spotlight had grown and I was no longer worthy of his friendship.

"Rumor, you're tripping." Taylor threw his phone to the ground and reached out to grab my hands, but I quickly pulled away. My tear ducts were growing thick with pain, and I didn't want Taylor to see me cry, so I stood to my feet and ran. I ran through the fog as my tears added to the fresh moisture of the misty ground. I was determined to not stop until I could no longer hear Taylor calling my name.

After a couple hours of walking alone with my thoughts, I found myself facing the lights of my home. My serenity had already been disturbed for the day, so it did not even bother me to hear the familiar sounds of arguing as I approached the house.

"This is stupid. I am a grown woman. I have the right to have my own views on the church," Gia shrieked.

"You sure do, so why don't you take your grown behind and find your own house. That way you can do and say whatever you want, whenever you want," said Aunt HoneyBea.

"Oh, please believe, I can't wait to move out of this old, dusty house anyway."

"Then what are you waiting for baby? Ain't nobody standing in your way."

"I can't afford my own spot right now, Auntie, you know that."

"Then that settles it. Put on your coat. You're going to men's day with me at the church," demanded Aunt HoneyBea just as I came walking through the front door. The tension within the house was so thick that I could barely breathe. Both of their angry eyes locked onto me as I stood within their line of fire.

"Take Rumor with you. She's not doing anything," Gia snapped.

"I didn't ask Rumor. I asked you."

"Auntie, I cannot support any institution that regards men as having inherent domination over women. We are just as strong as they are."

"Look, lil girl, ever since you started at that college, you've been walking around here spewing hatred on every man that you see. You did not learn that mess in my house, and you will not bring that mess back to my house."

"It's called the feminist movement. We do not hate men; we just believe that women are equal to men in every way. I am not going back to that church, and listen to them teach that a man should be the head of my household."

"First find you a household, then you can worry about that. Like I said, get your coat because you're going to church."

"But Auntie..."

"Lil Girl, you got one more time to 'but' me before I take a switch to that grown butt of yours." Aunt HoneyBea's voice switched to a tone that made it clear she was done arguing. Gia was known to push the envelope when it came to our Aunt's authority, but she also knew when she was on the verge of pushing too far.

As my aunt and cousin stood locked in an ultimate stand-off, I found myself standing awkwardly between the two of them. Gia did not utter one word, but she appeared as if she were struggling to hold in a full tirade of expletives. Aunt HoneyBea's fists trembled as if they were ready to unleash a thunderstorm of raining knuckles. I wanted to make a clear dash for my room, but in the midst of a hostile situation, I was afraid to make any sudden moves. I was stuck in between a rock and a very hard place until the sudden aroma of hair spray and perfume entered the house.

"Beatrice, honey, are you ready for church? I hear the men are introducing a new pastoral candidate." Said Sister Emmagene as she came sashaying through the front door.

"We're ready. Right, Gia?" Aunt HoneyBea shot Gia a look so mean, that I feared her eyes were going to burn a hole through my cousin's forehead.

"Great, cause I put on my good Spanx tonight and I only have a couple of hours before this can of biscuits decides to burst." Sister Emmagene cutely smiled and curtsied before returning to her car in the front yard.

"Lucky me, I'm being forced to go to a religious, sausage party with boughetto Barbie," said Gia sarcastically before stomping through the front door.

"God please give me the strength not to choke the life out of that child," said Aunt HoneyBea with a sigh.

"Auntie," I said as she turned to leave.

"Yes, baby."

"I don't want to be home alone tonight. Can I come?" I asked.

"Rumor, baby, you are so sweet. I wish that cousin of yours would learn a few things from you, but I thought you were staying here with your Aunt Mildred tonight."

"Aunt Mildred is sleep by 7 every night. I need to be around people right now," I explained.

"I can't argue with that. My sister sleeps more than a polar bear in heat. C'mon baby, let's go to church." Aunt HoneyBea threw her arm around me as we both walked out onto the front yard.

For the man-thirsty single women of Hurley, men's night was like the senior prom. They were all well-dressed to the tee in their most holy and righteous freak-um dresses. Sister Emmagene was like their leader as she sashayed towards the front row of the sanctuary. Gia curled her nose in disgust as Aunt HoneyBea forced us both to sit beside the desperate vixens.

As I sat down, I couldn't help but feel that someone was watching me. It was a feeling I had become very accustomed to with all of the drama surrounding my parent's lives. But at that point, my life had become old news to most of the people of Hurley. I turned my head just enough to get a view of the packed sanctuary. Everyone was so busy talking and greeting one another that none of them had any time to fixate on me. Well everyone with the exception of one man who sat on the very back pew. He barely stood out from the crowd as his complexion was nearly as dark as the shades covering his eyes. His stare was so focused that I could clearly feel him eyeing me even through the thick sunglasses. A black Kangol hat added even more mystery to his appearance. I knew there was no way that he was from Hurley, because men in Hurley knew better than to wear hats and shades in the church.

"Gia," I whispered to my cousin as she sat beside me pouting.

"What do you want?" said Gia, still fuming from having to attend.

"Check out the guy with shades and the black hat on the back row," I said.

"Girl, do not talk to me, especially not about no man. It's your fault that I'm stuck in this church on a Wednesday night anyway."

"How is it my fault?" I asked.

"Because you sat there like an ingrown hair on the infected

pimple that is my life and said nothing as Aunt HoneyBea forced me to come here. You could've volunteered then instead of after I was already trapped," Gia complained.

"That's ridiculous. Nothing I could have said would have changed auntie's mind about you coming to church."

"Well I guess that's the thing for tonight, because there's nothing you can say to make me say one more word to you. So shut up talking to me." Gia snapped.

As you can see, Deputy Ron Mack leaving Hurley left a stench on my cousin's attitude that I feared would never dissolve. Gia wouldn't admit that her new-found man hating philosophy had anything to do with Deputy Ron, but it was kind of obvious at that point. Instead of incurring any more of Gia's attitude, I turned to face the podium as Sister Sheila Owen emceed the Men's Night program.

"Good evening men and women of Hurley. I want to thank everyone for coming out tonight as we celebrate the heads of our homes, the protectors of our families, and the true rocks of our lives...our men." Sister Owen smiled and applauded along with the rest of the church. "Tonight, we will begin our service with a special musical and dance tribute from the women of the church. Then we will proceed with the uplifting of our anointed brothers who will be appealing to God's calling to become the next pastor of the Rock of the Delta First Missionary Baptist Church."

"Ugh, you could stab me in the chest with a rusty finger nail file and it would still be a more bearable death than listening to this mess," Gia groaned.

"I don't know. Let me reach in my bag and find this old fingernail file, because if you don't quit complaining, we're gonna put it to the test," Aunt HoneyBea threatened through clenched teeth.

I did not even dare glance at either my aunt or cousin as they quietly exchanged their frustrations. My mind was still puzzled by the unbending sensation of the mystery man's eyes burning holes into the back of my neck. Every few seconds I would glance into his direction, but he would never look away. I wasn't sure whether it was my imagination running away with me or not, but I could've sworn that he even smirked at me once. I was growing increasingly nervous with each second; that is until the insane tribute began.

The church was suddenly filled with loose feathers as women dressed in bird costumes danced across the stage. They squawked and flapped their arms like a bunch of mental patients. Three women dressed in all-white dresses cooed behind microphones from the background. Just when I thought the performance couldn't be any more ridiculous, the bird women rolled out a paper-Mache statue of a man on top of a little red wagon. The man's rib fell open as a scantily clad Sister Gibson tumbled out onto the stage.

I don't know why anyone was still surprised by Sister Gibson's antics, but the entire church gasped as she danced across the stage in a see-through leotard with leaves appropriately placed to hide her private parts. I could only assume that she was meant to be Eve, formed from the ribs of Adam. She hopped and danced across the stage like an untrained ballerina. Everyone sat and watched speechlessly as her leaves started to fall to the floor. Sister Gibson continued to dance like David, right out of her clothes.

"Well isn't that wonderful. Thank you, ladies." Sister Owen rushed out to the stage and interrupted what almost turned out to be Sister Gibson's exotic dance premiere.

"We aren't finished," Sister Gibson protested.

"Yes, you are. What is wrong with you, Mary? This is the church and there are children in those pews." Sister Owen attempted to whisper, but on the front row, we heard every word.

After the travesty that had just left the stage, no one expected anything worse, but we were quickly proven wrong as Sister Owen introduced the first pastoral candidate; his name was Brother Jebediah. He wore a bright purple, bell-bottomed suit with a golden Jesus-piece hanging from a chain which hung down to his belt. His stride was awkwardly confident as he took command of the stage.

"Let's give another round of applause for that beautiful rendition of the creation of man. Looking at Eve is proof enough that there is a God, Amen. Breasts and thighs, I say good Lord, Why? Hallelujah! Shekan Buya yay a wey!" Brother Jebediah shouted while speaking in tongues.

As I sat shaking my head at Brother Jebediah's sermon, my cell phone vibrated in my pocket. At first I assumed it was one of Taylor's apologies, but as I checked the screen I could see that it was none other than Tami Tahiri calling me. I know that it may be hard to believe that one third of my middle school nemesis could be calling me, but it was true. After Tasha and Tamicka both became pregnant, teenage dropouts, Tami latched on to me like a fly to feces. At first it was strange, and I tried like hell to avoid her, but it wasn't long before the last remaining Tahiri grew to become my only female friend.

"Auntie, I'm gonna go to the restroom." I lied, more than happy to free myself of having to view anymore of the evening's antics.

"Okay, baby," said Aunt HoneyBea as I excused myself from the church.

Before I could even say hello, Tami's voice screamed into my ear. "Chick, answer your phone. I got tea, girl! And I'm talking about Lipton Iced Tea!"

"Tami, I'm at church. I can't be listening to this gossip."

"Hold up, now. Now is not the time for you to be giving me attitude, because I got beef with you," said Tami.

"Girl, what is your problem?"

"You know how I feel about that cute ass Blaxican homeboy of yours. Mmm, girl, he could get it," said Tami nearly frothing at the mouth.

"Then maybe you should call him. We aren't on speaking terms right now," I said.

"What the hell did you do to my baby daddy? This is all your fault. I should've known," said Tami.

"You should've known what? Tami, I'm in church, I don't have time for this."

"Yes, you do. I hope you're sitting down, girl. This is some serious stuff."

"Spit it out already." I found myself growing irritated with Tami's rambling.

"Calm down! You don't just guzzle tea, girl. You have to sip it... slowly." Tami said calmly, knowing she was irritating me with anticipation. "Word on the street is that Taylor and that hoe Rima are back together."

"Typical. Not even two hours ago he was complaining about the girl. I'm so over it. Is that it?" I asked.

"I don't think you're ready for the rest of it." Tami teased.

"Tami, what is it?" I said, growing more impatient with each word.

"Well they say it's because she's two months pregnant with his child. Girl, he knocked her up. That heifer stole my man." Tami laughed, but I, on the other hand, could not find an inch of humor in the situation. My mind went silent. The shock of it all had completely consumed me. I couldn't feel the phone in my hand. It wasn't long before I couldn't feel my hands at all. My cell collapsed onto the ground in front of me. The light of the phone's screen dimmed to black. That screen was like my life; no matter how many times I found light, I always ended up in the dead of night.

I had no mother, and my father had never been mine. Taylor

was the one person who had always been meant for me. He was my best friend, and no one else's. Even though it may sound selfish, I always wanted him to myself. I always dreamt that he and I would fly with the butterflies for eternity, but that dream was no longer possible. If the rumors were true and he shared a child with Rima, my best friend would now be her baby's father for eternity. My heart was broken. I couldn't breathe. I fell to my knees. My face tightened with waves of sorrow. Before I knew it, I was crying out loud. My eyes were full of tears and my nose could not contain its mucus. I was a miserable mess.

Warm, panting breathes both nudged and blew my hairs away from my face. I pulled my devastated face away from the lines of my palms just in time to face the bluest eyes I'd ever seen on a creature. Its fresh tongue wiped the tears and mucus away from my face. I gripped the edges of its beautiful grey and white fur. It was like a gift from God sent just in time to save me from my own despair. It was a dog, a husky breed. He was large in size, but delicate in spirit. I continued to run my fingers through his comfortable coat of fur as he brushed his head against my own. His tail wagged back and forth like a free flowing pendulum.

"What are you doing out here alone, boy? Where's your owner?" I asked.

He stared back at me still with those unforgettable frosty, blue eyes. His tongue continued to glide against my hands and face. We had an instant connection. Somehow deep within my sadness, I managed to find a genuine smile.

An unexpected shift in a nearby hedge of bushes caused the dog's hairs to stand on edge. His tail no longer wagged with happiness. It froze stiff like a dried up tub of cement. He slowly turned to face the bushes with a low growl; he'd caught the scent of something or someone. Whatever it was, he didn't like it. I watched as he charged the bushes while barking furiously.

"That's some bark. I wonder how much trouble's in the bite." A very, dark figure stepped from beyond the bushes. His skin's tone nearly matched the shade of the night. His build was slightly broad and threatening. Both his bone structure and extremely pronounced features mixed to form an undeniably attractive, but at the same time, dangerous, appeal. As he stood facing off against the husky, I felt the weight of his presence weighing down upon my new-found friend.

Dogs have a unique way of sensing fear, but strangely, the mystery man felt none. He slowly approached the dog with a complete lack of hesitation. There was a sadistic level of confidence in his stride. The dog maintained its growl, but backed away from the man's overwhelming shadow. As the glimmer of the lunar lights peeked within the man's eyes, his smirk grew wide. The dog's growl calmed to a desperate whimper. Realizing he had gained the upper hand, the man jumped into a threatening stance and shouted. The dog yelped before turning and disappearing into the forest of trees surrounding the church.

"Why'd you do that? He wasn't bothering anyone," I cried.

"The Rumor Arden is out here crying on her knees in front of dogs and mosquitoes. This can't be the brave girl who single-handedly brought down a crime lord." He approached me while smiling, winking, and seductively wetting his lips. He wore a black leather trench coat and held a pair of shades and a Kangol hat in his right hand.

"You're the guy with the staring problem from the back row?" I asked.

"Good to know I can still leave an impression on a beautiful lady." He stretched out his massive hands to help me to my feet. I hesitated briefly before finally allowing him to help me up. There was an intriguing amount of strength in his grip that caused my nerves to shudder.

"Who are you?" I said while fully taking in his appearance. His tight eyes and strong jaw line made him a sight to be admired.

"Call me D."

"Ok, D., why are you following me?"

"Following you? Listen angel eyes, I just had to step out for a smoke break. This Black & Mild in my pocket was calling my name, if you know what I mean. I couldn't help but overhear your little problem," he said.

"So not only are you a stalker, but you're an eavesdropper as well. My little problem is none of your business."

"Now you're sounding like the kind of girl to beat down a boss. I can't front, I'm kinda turned on." He grinned slyly while stroking the hairs of his goatee with his fingertips.

"Oh my God, I'm going back to church. Please stay away from me," I said.

"Ok, but before you leave, what exactly are we going to do about your little problem? I think you'll find that I can be very useful when it comes to determining solutions."

"I don't remember asking for your help," I retorted.

"Well that never stops a gentleman from offering when he sees a lady in distress."

"Thanks but no thanks. I won't be requiring any services that you have to offer." I turned to walk away.

"That's fine, angel eyes. Just remember that these people will never respect you until you take what is yours. You can't always be their little victim."

"What are you talking about?" I asked.

"I've only known you about a good five minutes, and I can already tell that you're the perfect door mat," he said.

"Excuse you? You don't know me."

"But, you're wrong. I think I know you very well. I used to be you, angel eyes. I used to walk around trying to be nice to everyone.

I thought it would make people like me, but they'll never like you. You and me, we're what I like to call The Never Loved. No one really understands us, so we're always on the outside looking in. Trying to be seen and heard, but we'll never be seen. We'll never be popular. We'll never be heard," he explained. Although my guard was up, I couldn't help but relate to his words.

"Ok, I'll humor you for a minute. Even if you are right about what you're saying, what do you think you can do for me?" I asked.

"I can show you how to live, angel eyes. You see, you're just like your mother. She wanted them to accept her too. When she realized that she'd never be loved by them, she sacrificed her relationship with you, so that they'd love you. And now here you are lost among The Never Loved. You gotta do what your mother never had a chance to do."

"And what's that?"

"Live. Live your life the way you want to live it. Do you, angel eyes. Don't make your mama's mistakes. Trust me; you're different from everyone else. They'll never love you." As he spoke, his words hit me like a ton of bricks, but I refused to be influenced by the ramblings of a strange man. How dare he pretend to know anything about me? I had no idea what newspaper or magazine gave him the impression that he knew my story, but he didn't. He couldn't possibly know my struggle. Even though his words read like an introduction to my autobiography, I turned and walked away. Little did I know at the time, his words were somehow still following me.

Back in the church, Deacon Smith had taken the microphone. I could feel the importance of his message as his voice echoed throughout the halls, "Black men are under attack in America. The enemy has placed a target on us; a target that only the church can refute. Young, black men are being killed every other day by corrupt cops, and a system that was never meant to protect us has consistently failed to provide justice. God is not overlooking the spilled blood of his people. He is not ignoring our cries for help. He is waiting for us to call upon His name. Now is the time to call upon His name. Church say JESUS!"

As I returned to my seat, the church shouted in unison "JESUS!" Everyone applauded with the exception of Deacon Booker. He nervously shifted in his seat. I had no idea what that was about.

"Just as Herod failed to block your name, and just as Pharaoh failed the same, I'm calling JESUS! Rock the halls of Washington. Lord we are asking that you shake this system of wickedness and savagery against your people until it falls into Your will. Your people are calling upon Your name. Lord, You said that Your people, who are called by Your name and created for Your glory, and who You have formed and made shall lead the deaf and the blind. You said that nations shall assemble and know that You are God. You are Jehovah Jira, our provider; the One from whom we seek salvation. We are calling JESUS!" Deacon Smith shouted.

"JESUS! Halleluah!" the church screamed. The congregation wept and danced as the organs, pianos, and drums brought a level of excitement to the building. With so many black killings at the hands of corrupt officers there was tension building all across the nation. I could feel Deacon Smith's message leaving cracks in the sorrow of the church. He was giving us exactly what we all needed...hope.

The hope was so alluring that it was just as attractive to those outside of the four walls of the church. An unknown pair of ears was approaching to hear more. As he got closer, his presence was felt by the nose of Sister Annette Harris, who stood only a few yards away from me. At first she clapped against her tambourine with no worries in the world, but it wasn't long before her nose started to sniffle. She sneezed quietly, but soon her sneezes grew more powerful.

"Oh my Lord, what is going on in here? I haven't sneezed like this since..." she seemed confused as she pulled a Kleenex from her purse and wiped her nose.

"Sister, are you okay?" Brother Smith, one of the Men's Day ushers asked.

"No, it's as if there's a dog in here." Sister Annette Harris spoke the word dog, and my blue-eyed friend came rushing through the church as if he could hear her calling his name. Screams erupted from the pews, but these screams were not the screams of joy that we had heard earlier. The blue-eyed husky panted and barked with excitement as church-goers stumbled over pews trying to avoid him. I tried to get to him, but Aunt HoneyBea wasn't having it. She grabbed me and quickly yanked me aside.

"Auntie, please, I can help." I begged her to release me.

"Rumor, I am not letting you go play with that strange animal," said Aunt HoneyBea.

"Church, please remain calm." Deacon Booker stood to his feet as the ushers tried to catch the dog. Brother Smith was only inches away from grabbing him when the Husky heard my voice as I begged Aunt HoneyBea to let me go. Deacon Smith pounced, but the Husky leapt clean through his arms. With the dog still on the run, Deacon Smith fell onto Sister Haywood's wheelchair causing the wheel locks to disengage. Sister Haywood screamed as her chair rolled into the pulpit. The wheelchair hit the edges of the platform, shot forward onto its front two wheels and sent Sister Haywood flying into the Baptismal pool.

"Auntie, please," I said finally pulling myself from Aunt HoneyBea's grasp, but it was already too late.

The Husky leapt into my direction, but landed on Sister Emmagene's lap. Sister Emmagene panicked so wildly that her Spanx popped free of her waist. The extra-snug hosiery propelled from beneath her dress and boomeranged through the air like a Frisbee.

"Aahh, get this beast off of me!" cried Sister Emmagene, but every eye in the church was focused on the flying Spanx. It flew full speed ahead into Brother Hamilton, knocking him backwards into the organ. A tune of disaster played as the organ fell from the raised platform of the pulpit and broke in half with Brother Hamilton on top of it.

The church was finally silent as all eyes found the Husky sitting calmly in front of me. I rubbed against his soft fur to keep him warm. The anger projecting from their stares was almost too much to bear. The dog dropped his head into my legs, because even he could feel their anger descending onto the two of us.

"Topaz? Anybody seen my dog?" A man limped into the church pushing an old, rattling shopping cart. The cart was filled with blankets, clothes, and all kinds of other random items. He wore a filthy straw hat, a long and dingy fake fur coat, and overalls that covered a blue flannel shirt. His muddy boots left brown foot-prints on the church's carpet. Everyone gasped as the putrid, musty-smell of him flowed through each aisle of pews as he passed.

"This is ridiculous. You have ruined our Men's Day. Get your wolf and get out!" said Sister Sheila Owen fuming with anger.

"My apologies. Topaz is not used to being around so many people at once. I think he got a little excited." he said as Topaz raced into his embrace. I could tell that Topaz was overjoyed to see his master by the way he licked away at the man's face.

"Sir, please leave," said Deacon Booker.

"Oh, excuse my manners. I am Brother Markel Mickels. You can all call me Mickey. I'm here for the Men's Night. I hear there's an audition for those who have received God's calling to preach. I'm here at our Father's will." He explained.

"You fool! Can't you see that there is no Men's Night? Your dog destroyed it. Get out now!" Sister Owen screamed.

"Well, my apologies," he said while removing his straw hat and bowing slightly. "We'll be on our way. God bless you all. C'mon Topaz."

I watched each and every one of their disapproving stares as the man sadly left the church. I couldn't believe what I was seeing. It was just an accident. How could they all deny him entrance into God's house? My father would have never denied anyone entrance into the church. At that moment, I was reminded of D.'s warning. *"Trust me. You're different from everyone else. They'll never love you."*

They had proven D. to be right; Mickey wasn't like everyone else. They couldn't understand him, just as they would never understand me. We were both lost among the Never Loved.

Rumor's Journal Entry 1

Reflecting on what I've never had,
Making decisions I should never have,
Regretting my nature to be never bad,
Oh how I've wished to be never sad,
Or simply buy clothes I should never wear,
Nothing in common, I can never share,
They're only here when I'm never there,
No one understands, they will never care,
Always below, I'm never above,
Because there is no heaven on Earth...
for the Never Loved.

CHAPTER 3

The Tahiri Ride-Along
As Told By Rumor

The extreme blast of an engine backfiring combined with the loud tunes of gangster rap music made several birds scatter in all different directions. The flapping of frightened wings startled me out of a peaceful night's sleep. As a haze of fuel exhaust covered my window, I sighed deeply knowing that Tami Tahiri had arrived.

"Cough! Cough! Rumor, come out before your friend kills my flowers with all this smoke," Aunt HoneyBea yelled.

I wiped the previous night's sleep away from my tired eyes and jumped out of bed. I quickly brushed my teeth and threw my hair into a ponytail before walking into the kitchen to see Tami sitting comfortably in my seat at the breakfast table. She sat leaning back against the chair with her right foot resting on top of the table. Her high heel tapped against the table's edge as she excitedly shook her foot.

"Lil' girl, unless that foot is stamped grade A by the FDA, you'd be wise to remove it from my kitchen table. What's wrong with you Tahiri children? Ain't got no home training, that's your problem," Aunt HoneyBea fussed.

"My bad, Auntie. Rumor and I are about to leave anyway. Right, Rumor?" Tami smiled as I stepped into the kitchen.

"Going where? Tami, I'm tired." I said.

"Tired from what? You finally got one of them lil' d-boys to come blow out your back?" Tami joked.

"Chile, the only back being blown out in my house will be yours after I have to wriggle my foot from out of the crack of your behind. Take your lil' fast tail outside!" said Aunt HoneyBea.

"I was just playin', Auntie." Tami falsely apologized while suggestively rolling her tongue against the insides of her cheeks as my aunt turned her back.

"Tami, you are crazy. Come with me to the front yard before my auntie catches a charge,"

Aunt HoneyBea shot Tami a look of disgust as she rose from her seat. I could tell that she hated to see me hanging with someone like Tami, but with everything that had happened to me, she was also grateful to see me making friends. As hard as it was for Aunt HoneyBea, she bit her tongue and allowed me to hang with a Tahiri.

"Girl, I think Auntie is finally starting to warm up to me. This time I made it a whole ten minutes before she kicked me out of her house," Tami teased.

"Girl, please. She still can't stand you. She's just trying to be a good Christian." I said as we both sat down on the front porch facing Tami's 1995 Chevy Tahoe. The paint was chipped and rusted, and her front bumper had more dents than a mashed can of Play-Doh. But as ragged as the truck appeared, what puzzled me most was why she would put four shiny chrome rims on the tires.

"I see you checking out my new rims. I had my new man pimp out my ride." Tami smiled like a blushing little girl.

"Your new man? Since when do you have a man?"

"Uh uh, don't do that. Don't try and play me, Ms. Virgin. I gets mine," said Tami, wagging her pointer finger back and forth in front of my face.

"Whatever, Tami. Who is this man and when do I get to meet him?" I asked.

"That's why I'm telling you to go and put some clothes on. We're about to go see him."

"Really? You came all the way out here just to make sure I meet your new man?" I turned my lips up in disbelief.

"Okay, girl. You better not tell nobody. It's Jackson, one of the mechanics down at your uncle's new shop. We met at Walmart last weekend," Tami gushed.

"Tami, that man has to be at least 30 years old. What's wrong with you?"

"Age ain't nothin' but a number, boo. Besides, that man has an apartment and a credit card. I'm done fooling with these broke high school boys," said Tami, snapping her fingers and running them through her new quick weave.

"Girl, you are crazy. So you need me to pretend that you're taking me to the shop to see my uncle, so that you can visit your new boo on the low?"

"Ding, ding, ding! Now go put on some clothes and please do something with that hair. You ain't goin' nowhere with me looking like Aunt Jemima."

"Whatever. Don't worry about my hair. You just worry about getting Jackson to paint that rusty hoopty of yours." I laughed before running into the house to get dressed.

As I found a nice outfit and brushed my hair, Aunt Mildred came rolling into my room on her Hoveround scooter. Aunt HoneyBea had recently bought it for her birthday. My Aunt Mildred loved that scooter. If we weren't careful to watch her, she'd roll all throughout the streets of Hurley in that chair.

"Good Morning, Auntie," I said.

She mumbled a reply that I barely understood, "Good Morning Lieza."

"How was your sleep?" I asked. I loved when she called me Alieza. It was a beautiful reminder of how similar I was to my mother.

49

"Stay away from him, Lieza. He will hurt you." She grabbed my arm tightly and looked into my eyes with sincere anguish.

"Auntie, there is no he to stay away from." I said as she continued to squeeze my arm for dear life. She held on to me as if I were dangling from the edge of a mountain cliff.

"He will hurt you, Lieza. Lies!" she screamed.

"Ow, auntie you're hurting me!" I screamed while pulling away from her grip.

Aunt HoneyBea must've heard our screams, because she came rushing into my bedroom. "Mildred, get off of that child! Rumor, don't pay her any mind. It's those new meds the doctor's been giving her."

"Lies! Lies! Lies!" Aunt Mildred continued to scream as Aunt HoneyBea pulled her back into their bedroom. I hated when Aunt Mildred's condition got the best of her. I could tell that it hurt Aunt HoneyBea to see it as well. I took one look at my bruised arm and took a Deep breath before dressing for the trip with Tami.

Meanwhile, on the front steps, my cousin Gia had encountered Tami. I had no idea what to expect from two mean girls coming together. As I moved closer to the front door, I could see Gia standing with her arms folded. Tami, on the other hand, sat with her legs crossed. I could not hear what they were saying, but I ran to the porch just in case.

"O.M.G., girl! Those heels are everything," said Gia.

"Girl, I know, I just had to get them. They were on sale at Sear's," said Tami.

"Really? How did I miss that sale?" asked Gia.

"Mmmmm, it was a limited time, five-finger Tahiri discount," Tami laughed.

"You are so crazy. I like you. What are you doing hanging with that lame lil' cousin of mine?" asked Gia.

"I'm ready, Tami. Gia mind your business," I said while relieved to see that they were actually getting along.

"Well anyway, take this flyer. You seem like a strong, I-N-D-E-P-E-N-D-E-N-T chick, if you know what I mean. We at the She-Man feminist group will be meeting on campus at Hurley Community College. You should come," said Gia before rolling her eyes in my direction and heading into the house.

As the door closed behind Gia, Tami scrunched the flyer into a ball and threw it into the back of her truck. "Chile, please. Your cousin is cool and all, but Tami doesn't go anywhere where there will be no men present. C'mon, Rumor."

Tami drove her huge truck just as well as any man. I watched in amazement as she whipped the wheel of that truck in and out of lanes. She was driving like a bat straight out of hell as she sped through traffic. If I hadn't known any better, I would've sworn we were flying. With the exhaust from her over-heated engine and the way the road lines blurred beneath her speed, everything seemed to be fading around me. I held onto my seatbelt for dear life. The rapid back and forth motion was leaving me a little sea sick. I looked over at Tami, and she sat calmly as if the car was barely moving.

"Tami, you're killing me over here," I said.

"What are you talking about? I'm only doing about 60," said Tami.

"Sixty what? Miles over the speed limit?" I said sarcastically.

"You're damn right," Tami laughed while continuing to hustle across the highway like a fugitive on the run from the law.

"I swear I'm never riding with you again," I grumbled.

"What's your problem? We out here riding. I know exactly what you need," said Tami as she smirked and turned the nob of her car radio. Before I knew it, the loud bass of old school Lil' Kim came bursting through her amps and speakers. My entire body pounded from within as several waves of beats consumed me.

But, I turned off the radio; knowing that the only way to

distract Tami from her music was to switch her focus to her men. "Ok, enough of that. Tell me more about how you met Jackson."

"So I was at Walmart, right? I was trying to find some neutralizer for my perm. By the way, you didn't say anything about my new Quick Weave. Girl, I know I'm rocking this burgundy hair," said Tami while running her fingers through her hair. She was pretty in a very hard kind of way. She had a light complexion with cheekbones so sharp they could cut through rubber. She had a long, slender nose, thick lips and was wearing a dark shade of maroon lipstick. But it was her eyes that added to her rough exterior. They were dark and tight and gave the appearance of a scowl even when she was smiling. It was a trait that she shared with her sisters, and definitely one of the reasons no one wanted to be on the wrong side of a Tahiri.

"It's beautiful, now tell me more about Jackson," I said trying to keep her focused on the story.

"Right! Girl, I couldn't find that neutralizer anywhere. I asked this little, old lady for some help. She looked at me like I was speaking Spanish. I was like girl don't start none, won't be none. I ain't come all the way to Walmart to be catchin' no cases," Tami continued.

"Is Jackson coming into the story anytime this decade?" I asked, temporarily interrupting her bout of incoherent rambling.

"I'm getting there. What did I tell you about tea? You'd better learn to sip," said Tami. "Anyway, as I was saying, before I was rudely interrupted, the old lady gave me attitude for no reason. I turned around and let her ass have it. Girl, I read her like she was the bible. Then all of a sudden, I felt this strong hand, smelling of hard-working-man-musk tap my shoulder. It was love at first sniff."

"And it was Jackson?" I said relieved that we were finally reaching the point of her story.

"Nah, it was the muffin man who lives on Drury Lane," Tami

said sarcastically. "Of course it was Jackson, with his fine self. Girl, I turned around and that man was talking to me, but I couldn't hear one word that was coming out of his mouth. The only thing I could focus on was his chest muscle cleavage staring back at me from underneath his wife beater. That shirt stuck to him harder than a wet paper napkin. Uh! I'm having palpitations just thinking about it."

As Tami spoke, I noticed that we were entering Mercy Projects. I had only been to Uncle Champ's new shop a few times, but I was sure that it was nowhere near Mercy Projects. I shot Tami a look of confusion that she immediately picked up on.

"Don't worry, Rumor. I need to make a stop real quick. We won't be here long," she said. Tami knew exactly how I felt about Mercy Projects. I hadn't been back to the place since my mother's death. I hated having to revisit those memories.

We came to a stop in front of an apartment with a clique of alley-acting thugs howling as if we were cattle and they were blood thirsty wolves. Their antics didn't scare Tami one bit. She unbuckled her seat-belt and opened the door as if she'd been to the place many times before. I grabbed her arm and shot her a serious look of concern.

"Chill, Rumor. I got this. Just lock the doors. I'll be back in a second," said Tami before shutting the truck's door.

I watched as she switched the hips of her hour glass figure. Tami's walk was one that had been known to melt the hearts of most men. Sometimes I envied her confidence and fearless attitude. I wanted to know what it was like to be a Tahiri for just one day, because it must've been an amazing feeling to live each day without the fear of consequences.

Tami came to a stop in-between the group of boys. They all eyed her behind like it was a piece of ribeye steak, but she wasn't intimidated at all. I watched as she twisted in place, giggled, and threw her hair backwards over her shoulder. They all loved her flirtatious demeanor, and she unapologetically fed off of their attention. It was an intriguing sight to say the least. Then I watched as she carefully pulled a small bag from her hip pocket. One of the boys, who sat facing her, stood and grabbed her hand. He planted a delicate kiss on the back of her hand before releasing it from his grip. Tami turned and sashayed back towards the truck as if nothing had happened.

"Did you just sale him a bag of..." I attempted to ask.

"You didn't see anything. Now let's go see your uncle." Tami cranked up her engine and we zoomed off with a cloud of exhaust. As curious as I was, I didn't ask another question about her hood transaction.

For a moment, we rode in complete silence until Tami decided to spark conversation with some local gossip. "Girl, I heard about what happened at the church yesterday. Why didn't you tell me that crazy old homeless man and his dog destroyed the church? They say Miss Emmagene's Spanx popped off like a wine cork."

"Yeah, it was horrible what they did to that poor man and his dog," I said.

"What did they do to him?" asked Tami.

"They kicked him out of the church."

"Girl, I can't even remember the last time I've been to anybody's church, but even I don't believe the church is a place for street trash."

"Being homeless makes him a street rat? That's not cool, Tami. We don't know anything about that man's struggle. But what I do know is that anybody's struggle is more than enough reason that they should be in somebody's church."

"Yeah, I guess you're right. Girl, look at this tacky trucker over here trying to check you out." Tami intentionally changed the subject of our conversation, but I looked out of my window and saw an overweight man behind the wheel of an 18-wheeler. Tami was right. He was disheveled and creepy as he licked his greasy lips at me.

"Eww, between your driving and this perv to my right, I'm about to lose my lunch." I said.

"Well I know how to solve at least one of those problems." Tami smiled before pressing her gas pedal all the way down to the floor. I felt my head jerk backwards into the seat as we took off.

"What are you doing?" I screamed.

"About to give that freak show something to look at." Tami had a maniacal look in her eyes; it was a look that meant she was up to no good.

The trucker took the revving of Tami's engine as a dare to race. My ears went numb as his engine blasted with hers. The wind whipped against my face like the blades of a giant fan. I continued to scream, but my voice was among the many sounds that were lost to the blasting of their engines. All I could do was sit there and nervously watch as my life flashed before my eyes.

The 18-wheeler's cargo truck lashed in and out of our lane as Tami skidded across the road to avoid the impact. Not once did she decrease her speed. Rocks and pebbles shot across the car from all directions. The driver looked down on us with laughter as the smoke cloud continued to build behind us. His crooked teeth gave me the sensation of a real horror story. I dug my fingers so Deeply into Tami's car seat that I could feel the leather beneath my nails.

Tami's eyes were focused on the road. Her burgundy weave blew behind her head like dragon's breathe. Her beady eyes tightened with a level of determination that was equally as frightening as the trucker's crooked teeth. I screamed for her to slow down, but by the look of her thigh muscles flexing, Tami was not going to lighten the pressure on the accelerator.

In my mind, I could see us crashing into the median with smoke and flames gathering around us like the devil's minions. I saw myself flying from the car like a rock from a sling-shot. Fire and darkness lashed against my face. Just as the hard trunk of a large tree dominated my view, my heart nearly stopped. I gasped my last breath before everything went black.

"After I leave you two ladies in my dust, I think I'll wave your panties as my victory flag." The trucker's voice managed to blow into my ears and break my nightmare into pieces. I was still alive, but Tami was even more determined to beat the trucker. We were moving with dangerous speed.

"How about you hang that ball sack that you call a chin, you fat bastard?" Tami screamed in retaliation.

His wise talk seemed to be an extra tank of gas for her truck, because I swear we reached speeds that were not even recorded on the speedometer. The trucker's eyes bulged as we started to gain ground on him. We were only feet away from passing him. I continued to grip the seats with all of my strength as a giant pothole came into view.

"Tami, watch that pothole!" I screamed, but she was so caught up in the race that she could not hear one word I said.

Our tires slammed into the pit of the pothole so hard, that the entire truck ejected into the air. The truck rotated 360 degrees in mid-air before landing about two feet ahead of the 18-wheeler. My heart felt as if it were about to beat right out of my chest. Tami, on the other hand, did not miss a beat. She pulled her car directly in front of the 18-wheeler. He slammed on his breaks and lost control of his vehicle. The cargo behind his truck swung out as he skidded across both lanes. I could tell that the man was yelling all kinds of curse words as we sped off into the distance.

"I always suspected it, but now I know for sure that you have lost your mind. You could've killed us!" I cried as Tami finally slowed her truck down.

"Quit trippin', Rumor. I do this for a living." Tami bragged.

"You are not Dale Earnhardt, and this is not NASCAR. Don't you ever do that again!"

"Okay, mama Rumor, calm down."

"I can't believe this. I saw my entire life flash before my eyes." I desperately panted for air.

"It wasn't that bad."

"No, it was definitely worse. But the crazy thing is all I could see was Taylor. He's been there for me, my entire life. I can't just check out on him now when he needs me most." I confessed.

"It's about time you came to your senses. Jackson is cool and all, but I'm gonna need my baby's Daddy back in the picture too," Tami joked.

"Girl, you are so..." before I could even finish my sentence, Tami's engine blew. It was a blast much louder than the sound I was used to hearing from her car. The car stalled a few times before stopping completely in the middle of the road.

Tami turned and looked at me awkwardly. She could tell that I was heated. "So you still love me right, Rumor?"

"Aaagh!" I screamed.

The sun had set and the night was starting to stretch across the sky. My feet were aching and my head was throbbing. I couldn't believe the day we'd had. We had been walking for miles since we left Tami's truck. I didn't speak one word to her throughout the entire walk. I was infuriated until we finally made it over a steep hill and a rest stop came into view.

I was so thirsty that I tackled the water fountain as soon as I saw it while Tami rushed into the women's restroom. The water felt like the breath of life as it flowed into my body. I relished in every single drop of it.

"Excuse me, Ma'am. I think you owe me a victory wave." The low groan of a man's voice whispered into my ears. I turned to see the disgusting trucker from earlier.

"Umm, I think you have me confused with someone else, sir." I said.

"No ma'am. One thing about me is I never forget a pretty face," he said while pushing his repulsively soft stomach against me.

"I'm about to leave now, so please move." My nerves were getting the best of me. I tried my best to be intimidating, but my voice both shook and cracked as he descended upon me.

"Get off her, fool!" Tami came out of the bathroom like a whirlwind. She jumped on the large man's back and pounded her fists against his head. He squealed like the fat pig that he was as she dug her nails into his face. He then pushed himself backwards into the wall, smashing Tami between himself and the brick structure. Tami dropped to the ground while gripping her back with pain.

"Get over here!" he yelled while pulling me to the ground beside Tami. He peered down on us from his wide, scratched face and his crooked teeth. I held Tami's hand as she continued to writhe with pain. "You two almost made me destroy my truck. Well, it's okay, you're about to make it up to me real soon. Let's play."

"I don't think they're in the mood. How about you come play with me?" A man with a very familiar voice tapped the trucker from behind. The trucker turned to face him just in time for the man to uppercut him directly into his bloated chin. Tami and I both jumped aside as the large tub of lard fell backwards onto the brick wall. I looked up to see none other than D. with his arm stretched outward to help us both to our feet.

I never thought I'd be so happy to see the man who was ogling me in church, but D. was definitely a sight for sore eyes. So much had happened that day that I couldn't find the correct words to speak so I was silent as D. ushered us both to his car. Tami, on the other hand, knew all of the right words; and she wasn't holding back.

"My hero, you are so damn fine. Please marry me," she not so subtly flirted.

"I'm no hero. I just got a job at Mr. Champ's shop up the street from here, and I overheard him on the phone with your aunt. She was worried that something had happened to you girls. She said you'd left hours ago, and you were supposed to be coming to the shop. I volunteered to come looking for the two of you," D. explained.

"Well baby, you can look for me anytime," said Tami. "Has anybody ever told you that you look like a young Morris Chestnut? Be my best man, baby."

"You're funny as hell," D. laughed. "How about you, Angel Eyes? Are you okay back there?"

I could see him eyeing me through his rear-view mirror. All I could do was shrug my shoulders in reply. I was grateful for D.'s help, but I was having a very hard time processing the day's events.

After finally reaching my uncle's shop, I swiftly darted into his arms. I hugged him and cried. I cried for my friendship with Taylor. I wept for Mr. Mickey and his dog. Then I cried more for Aunt Mildred, and I totally lost control of my tears when I realized how much I was missing my mother.

"Don't cry, baby girl. I'm gonna get you and your friend home," said Uncle Champ.

"Can you take me somewhere else first? I have something that I really need to do," I said.

"Anything for my Rumor," Uncle Champ replied.

It was pretty late when we arrived at Taylor's house. I had to see him before I would ever be able to get any sleep. Life was too short, and I definitely owed him an apology.

"You want me to go in with you, baby girl?" Uncle Champ asked.

"No, I should do this alone. I'll be back in a minute," I said.

As I walked toward Taylor's house, my legs felt like cement bricks. I was terrified at the possibility that I may have pushed away my best friend for good. I didn't know what I would do without him. As their front porch light shined into my eyes, I fought hard to hold back my tears. Before I could even knock, the door opened and Taylor's mom, Ms. Louise Vazquez, stood before me.

"Come in, Rumor. Taylor took out some trash to the cans in the backyard. He should be back soon," said Ms. Vazquez.

"Thank you. How are you, Ms. Vazquez?" I said.

"Same as usual. Just tired from work and school. How is everything going with you and your family? I hear they're looking for a new pastor at the church," she said.

"Yeah, it's gonna be pretty hard to replace my dad."

Louise became very quiet after that. I could see her shoulders trembling while her back was turned towards me. I touched her shoulders to see if she was okay, but she quickly slapped my arm away.

"Ms. Vazquez, did I say something wrong?" I asked.

"Of course not, you never say anything wrong. How the hell am I supposed to hate you when you never say anything wrong?"

"I don't understand."

"You think I don't realize the way you and your family look down on me, Rumor. You don't think I see the judgment in your eyes every time that you come around here," Louise cried.

"I'm not judging you." I said.

"You're always judging me!" she screamed. "You did this to me. I could've been so much better. Lucky was my man! He loved me until she tricked him and became pregnant with you. Taylor was supposed to be his son. My life was never supposed to be this way. You stole everything from me, even my own damn father."

I couldn't believe the stuff that she was saying. I never imagined that she felt that way about me. Taylor and I had been friends almost our entire lives. What was causing Louise to say such hurtful things?

"I'm not sure what's going on here, but I'm about to leave. Please tell Taylor that I came by," I said.

"Yes, leave. Please leave my son alone. You Arden's are toxic to my family. Just leave us alone. If you care anything about my son, then please let him be happy without you in his life." Louise said before opening the front door to let me out. My eyes filled with tears as Taylor stood on the other side of the door.

"Rumor," I could tell that he was so elated to see me. His reaction was perfect, but I had already been hurt by the reality of Louise's words. The last thing I wanted to do was hurt Taylor. I was so confused, so all I could do was run. I ran past Taylor while pushing him aside. I didn't stop until I was back in my Uncle's truck. Taylor came running towards the truck after me.

"What's going on, baby girl?" Uncle Champ asked.

"Just please drive." I cried.

"But isn't that your friend?" Uncle Champ continued to question.

"Please drive," I said. I took one look at Taylor's face; he appeared to be so confused. I wanted to reach out to him. I wanted to embrace him, but also in my view, I could see Louise glaring at me. I turned my head away from them both as Uncle Champ reluctantly drove away.

Rumor's Journal Entry 2

No hope for the lost,
But no loss for the driven.
Trying to turn my page,
But the words have not been written.
Now I hold the pen,
But I don't know where to begin.
A feeling is uneasy within,
I fear I've lost my best friend.
But how can I ever win,
If my love for him is among my greatest sins?

CHAPTER 4

Nappy Roots
as Told by Rumor

For a girl, there aren't many situations more frustrating than a bad hair day, especially when your hair is as thick as mine. Even my pillow seemed to cringe after spending an entire night beneath my disturbingly matted hair. With the crust of sleep still blocking my eyes, I desperately used my hands to locate my hair comb. The random contents of my junk drawer rolled freely across the wooden surface until I pulled out something small, hard, and cold. I wiped the crust from my eyes just in time to see the last remaining black cat diamond. I quickly shook my hands free of the diamond as if it were a burning ball of metal. I couldn't explain why I secretly held on to the remnant of darker days. Sometimes, I felt like the little girl who used to purposely open healing wounds just to feel the forgotten pain. I pulled my comb from the drawer and immediately pushed it shut. Unfortunately, I was still able to look into the mirror and face the beginning of my struggle hair day.

As I sat before my vanity mirror, I struggled to pull the comb through my newly grown roots. The kinky, nappy hairs took such a strong hold of my comb that they ripped three teeth clean off of it. I hated fighting with my hair. The wild, rough mane of wool on my head only served as an everyday reminder of my inadequacies.

I was going to have to visit Sister Emmagene's shop after school. I needed an emergency treatment soon.

While facing my reflection, I couldn't help but reflect on a memory of more nappy days. I was only four years old and I admired my mother's hair. It was so long and silky smooth as it flowed across her shoulders, and that was long before I knew anything about a perm. I just remembered that she would always brush through her hair with such ease. I wanted to be just like her, so I foolishly sought out the help of my cousin Gia.

Even as a small child, Gia never missed an opportunity to torture me. That day I became her little science project. I remember standing in front of this same vanity staring at a head full of combs, brushes, barrettes, spoons, wrenches and all sorts of other household appliances tangled inside of my hair. All of the heavy houseware pulled so roughly against my scalp. It felt as if each of my hairs was being yanked from the follicles. I cried out in pain, but the more I cried, the louder Gia laughed. She fell backwards onto her back while screaming with laughter.

"Gia, what are you doing to my child?" My mama gasped at the sight of my hair.

"I didn't do anything. She did it." Gia lied.

"Please don't make me hurt you about my child," said mama as she frantically pulled the heavy items out of my hair.

"And I'll tell Aunt HoneyBea. You can't touch me. You ain't my mama." snapped Gia.

"You know what, Gia? You're right." My mama calmly spoke while kneeling down to face Gia. "I won't do a thing. I just want you to know the truth about the noises that you always hear at night. You know that noise that HoneyBea always tells you is loose pipes?"

"Yea, what about it?" asked Gia.

"Those pipes aren't loose, but the boogie monster is. Sleep with one eye open," mama said.

"You're lying. There's no such thing as a boogie monster," said Gia.

"Fine, believe what you want. I'm just trying to warn you. Why do you think so many of your Barbie dolls keep coming up missing? He's confusing them for you. Just think about it." My mama smiled before turning back to my head.

Gia's eyes shifted suspiciously. Even though she wanted to believe there was no boogie man, her youthful imagination quickly took hold of the idea. She tried to maintain her courage, but the seed of fear had already been planted. She was scared. She had always wondered why she kept losing so many dolls. Her eyes filled with so many tears that it wasn't long before she went running to find our aunt.

"Mama, it hurts," I cried as she brushed the rubble of Gia's mischief from my hair.

"Baby, why did you let your cousin do this to you?" she asked.

"I wanted to be pretty like you, mama," I answered.

"Listen to me, baby girl. You are beyond beautiful. Your beauty has nothing to do with hair or clothes. It's inside of you. It's like a light that no one can ever put out," she said while massaging her fingers through my scalp. Her hands were like magic as they soothed the sore areas.

Thinking back on that moment, I couldn't help but to miss her. I missed her so much. When you miss someone, everything reminds you of the time that you've spent with them. It was kind of like my current dilemma with missing Taylor. I can't watch television without wanting to call Taylor and talk about our favorite shows. I can't even listen to music because we both loved all different genres of songs. I'm even disturbed by the sight of butterflies. I feel like I'm always walking around with both eyes closed because when I open them, the people that I'm missing are all that I ever see.

As I listened to Gia stomp down the hallways outside my

bedroom door, I finally realized that what I was feeling must've been only a taste of the pain that was eating away at her. As mean and hard as she could be, Gia was a very sensitive person. Watching her as she struggled with her moods, it was painfully obvious that time does not heal all wounds. She'd gone years without seeing Ron Mack. My cousin was fighting a fight that she could not help but to lose.

"I'm moving out," said Gia as she faced Aunt HoneyBea with a blank expression. There was no life in her eyes, not even the singe of attitude that had become her trademark.

"Gia, I don't have time for jokes. Come over here and help me skin this fish." Aunt HoneyBea did not look up once from the sink full of raw fish that she planned to cook.

"I'm not joking, auntie. My feminist group is initiating a new program; where only a few special women, like me, live in one building and swear off all unnecessary contact with men," Gia explained.

"Hold on, let me get this straight. You're about to become a non-Catholic Nun?" Aunt HoneyBea laughed.

"Ugh, it's not funny. You have no respect for my choices. I'll be out of your house by the end of the week," said Gia.

"Child, calm down. What about your schooling?" Aunt HoneyBea asked.

"I'll still attend my regular classes. I just can't be around men during my down time," said Gia.

"But what about your family? Your Uncle Champ? Gia, what about your brother, Darryl Junior?" Aunt HoneyBea continued to question.

"Darryl Junior has his own family now. He, Chrisette, and the baby moved away over a year ago. We barely ever see them anyway. Uncle Champ doesn't need me. Everybody's doing their own thing, Auntie. It's time I do mine," said Gia.

"I'm sure your mother is rolling over in her grave knowing the decisions that you're making." Aunt HoneyBea's cheerful disposition quickly turned sour. As much as she and Gia butted heads, I don't believe she ever considered there would come a time when Gia would not be around.

"She's dead, Auntie. She's gone, just like my baby and the man that I..." Gia paused just as her emotions caused her voice to break. She clasped her mouth with both her hands and sighed deeply.

"Gia, baby, I know you're hurting. Let your family be here for you," said Aunt HoneyBea fighting back tears.

Gia was speechless. She only shook her head and squinted as tears streamed down her face. She turned and ran into me just as I was leaving my bedroom. I fell backwards into the hallway wall, and watched with confusion as she descended into the basement.

"What's wrong with her?" I asked.

As if it had heard my question, the kitchen television transitioned to a special broadcast announcement: "New Orleans rookie police officer, Ronald Mack, is making national headlines this week as he has reached out to the parents of the young man, Nicholas Macon, who was shot down by an unknown police officer. The Macon family was so touched by Officer Mack's words that they have teamed up to start a community initiative that will repair the relationship between the city's protestors and its local police force. Stay tuned as we will be sharing more details later in the hour."

"My Lord, that news has got to be where all of this is coming from. God bless her heart because no matter how far she runs, she can't escape this," said Aunt HoneyBea sadly.

I would soon learn just how correct my aunt really was when she said there are some problems that we can't outrun. With a headband covering my newly grown hair roots, I stood at the bus stop waiting for my big yellow ride to school. It was the first day of school after a much needed break, and I was so nervous about having to face Taylor again. A part of me just wanted to bury my head in the sand and never return to the surface, but those flashing red lights and that moving stop sign made it clear that trouble had arrived.

"Quiet back there!" our bus driver, Mrs. Thelma Haze shouted. Her fiery, raspy voice cut through the loud, post pubescent noise of the school bus like a butcher knife.

I hated that my bus stop was among the last few on Mrs. Haze's route. I felt like a prisoner of war as I walked down the aisle of rambunctious teenagers. My ears ached beneath the impact of their loud shouting and stomping. All of their eyes shifted back and forth between Rima and I as she sat confidently waiting for me to walk past her. Rima and her crew seemed untouchable as flying spit balls and all sorts of juvenile antics flew all around them but never crossed their paths. She and her girls were called The Lix, a name that was characterized by their constant licking of lollipops. The boys all loved it, but as I approached the sugar-tongued beauties, their uniform candy craze seemed creepy to me.

Taylor sat beside Rima with his head facing the floor; he couldn't even look in my direction. I felt horrible for the way everything had turned out between us. I wanted to reach out to him, but I could barely even think over all of the noise on the bus.

"Ok MTV, check out this lil' nobody right here. That's Rumor Arden. We hate that heifer. Ain't that right, Rima?" Candace, Rima's best friend, leaned forward with her knees planted against the bus seat. The red light of her large camcorder shined into my eyes.

"Right! She's so lame," Rima added after pulling a red lollipop from her mouth.

"Rima, chill," Taylor whispered without lifting his head once.

Natalie, the final member of the Lix crew chimed in. "She's a hater. She wants to be Rima so bad. She even tried to take Rima's boyfriend, lying about being his friend. Boys can't be just friends with chicks. Everyone knows that."

"What's this; some kind of audition for the Meatball Mistresses of Mississippi or is MTV suddenly interested in finding Snooki rejects?" I folded my arms across my chest while rolling my eyes at Candace's camera.

"Cut! Who let wack chicks on the set?" Natalie shouted.

"Girl, bye." I said while shoving Candace's camera aside to find me a seat. But as her camera was thwarted, her foot slid in front of my next step. Before I knew it, I tripped over her foot and fell flat on my face. The entire bus screamed with laughter.

Taylor jumped across Rima to help me up, but just as I was almost on my feet, Rima shrieked, "Ow, the baby."

"Rima, are you okay?" Taylor quickly released me and turned to check on Rima.

"All of this stress is just too much for the baby," Rima pouted while rubbing against the small lump on her lower belly.

"I don't believe this," I sighed and wiped the hair away from my eyes.

"Sit down, Rumor," Mrs. Haze screamed like a wounded bat. The three Lix laughed hysterically as I continued on through the bus to find a seat.

I was never a fan of school, but there were no words to describe how much I hated having to walk into Hurley High School without my best friend by my side. I felt so alone. The schoolyard was cliquish as usual. The Lix all sat together gossiping and slurping on their cavity sticks. Taylor and the rest of the basketball team dribbled the ball up and down the parking lot while bragging about their skills and girls. The crew of D-Boys threw dice and dollar bills across the parking lot while shouting random profanities. The Band crew compared instruments and contemplated on the adventures of their summer camp. The smart kids sat in a huddle, studying for absolutely no reason at all. The cheerleaders posted against a wall and set the perfect thirst traps for random boys. There was a place for everyone, but me. The only friend I had left was Tami, and she never showed up to school until at least fifteen minutes after the last bell every morning.

Coach Khaled's whistle echoed across the school yard as he disrupted the games of the gambling D-Boys. "Break this mess up. I'll be confiscating this cash. Get to class."

"Ay man, coach, classes don't start until after the bell rings," one of the D-Boys shouted.

"Well, go find something productive to do. I'm still taking this money. Your lil' bad asses don't need it, and my car note's due. They don't pay me enough for this mess," complained Coach Khaled before setting his sights on me.

"Hey there, lil' Rumor. How's your Uncle Champ doing these days? I hear he's got a new shop on the other side of town." Coach's Khaled's lanyard full of key chains jingled loudly as he stepped before me.

"Yes sir, he's doing great," I answered briefly, not really in the mood for small talk.

"You got a number for the shop? A few of the school busses are acting up. Principal Cheadle wants to set up a contract with a mechanic to have them fixed," Coach Khaled continued.

"Sure." I answered as I pulled out my cell phone to find my uncle's number. I could feel the Lix eyeing me. They were no doubt concocting some sort of gossip about the Coach and me. I was so beyond ready for the day to be over.

"Preciate that, lil' Miss Rumor," said Coach Khaled before turning to blow his whistle at the basketball team. "Get out of the parking lot before you fools hit my car."

As I watched the basketball team scrambling across the yard with Coach Khaled in hot pursuit, Taylor and I made brief eye contact. His eyes were questioning me. They wanted to know why I let our friendship go, but all I could do was look away. I couldn't explain what I, myself, didn't understand. Louise's words frightened me. I couldn't help but think that maybe he was better off without me and my drama.

"I'm so tired of you always looking at my man." I looked down to see shadows of the Lix stretching across my own. The three of them stood behind me as Rima spoke.

"Rima, I really don't feel like doing this with you today. Please leave me alone," I said while turning to face them. It was always weird to me how hateful someone as beautiful as Rima could be. With long, naturally curly, auburn colored hair flowing across both her shoulders, Rima cut the cutest pair of hazel eyes in my direction. She had the brightest skin I'd ever seen on a black girl. Candace and Natalie, on the other hand, were not as naturally beautiful. Like other girls in the school, they wanted to look like Rima, but unlike the other girls, they knew how to replicate her looks. They covered their faces in tons of make-up to brighten their complexions. They wore contacts to color their eyes, and weave extensions to mimic Rima's hair. They were like her clones as they stood to her side matching her every movement and mannerism. It was like watching The Stepford Wives in 3D.

"Aww, she wants us to leave her alone. How cute. She's not so tough without her Tahiri bodyguard, is she?" Natalie giggled.

"I don't need Tami to handle my problems, okay!" I snapped.

"Girl, please, just watch yourself when it comes to my man. We have a child on the way, so I'd appreciate it if you'd step off. Besides, look at me and look at you. You're sitting there with a played-out headband covering your kinky ass hair. Girl, go find a perm and mind your nappy-headed business," said Rima before turning to walk away with her two followers close behind.

"Oooh girl, that was a good take. MTV's going to eat this

footage up." Candace raved while replaying the footage of Rima confronting me.

As the bell finally rang to signal the beginning of first period, I self-consciously brushed against my hair with my hands. I had no idea that my bad hair day was so obvious. I cringed at the thought of continuing my day with a tragedy unfolding across my scalp. My head was weighed down with shame as I reluctantly proceeded to my first class.

As if my day hadn't already been crappy enough, I hurried down the school's hallway just in time to discover that my locker was jammed shut. I pulled and yanked against that lock with all of my strength, but it wouldn't budge. I could feel all of that day's frustrations mounting within me as I continued to fight with the stubborn locker. The hallway was nearly empty as everyone else had already made it to class. I, on the other hand, lost all track of time as I pummeled against my locker door. I screamed and cursed erratically, unleashing a tirade of anger that was meant for Rima, Louise, and the creepy fat trucker. Until that moment, I hadn't realized exactly how much anger I had been holding in. I was like a volatile volcano that was primed for eruption. The pain of banging my fists against steel eventually became too much for my knuckles. I turned around with my back against the locker and slowly slid to the ground. I sobbed uncontrollably. They weren't tears of sadness or joy, just salty droplets of rage flowing down each of my cheeks.

"Damn, my nugget. You beat that locker like it stole your last slice of government cheese." I followed the sound of a voice up to the reddest pair of eyes I'd ever seen. They were eyes so red that they clearly belonged to none other than Hakeem "Highlighter" Harris. Everyone called him Highlighter because Hakeem would sniff on anything that might give him a high, including chalk, markers, glue, crayons, hand sanitizer, and of course, highlighters. He had a pretty big crush on me for as long as I could remember, but that wasn't really saying much seeing as how he probably sniffed away his last good brain cell years ago.

"The stupid thing won't open. I'm tired of this stupid locker in this stupid school on this stupid day," I screamed.

"Calm down, Rumor. Sounds like a good girl needs a little pharmaceutical if you know what I mean," he said while reaching into his book bag full of school supplies.

"I don't want to sniff on any glue, Highlighter. I'll be fine. Just leave me alone," I said.

"Glue? C'mon my nugget. It's a new year and I'm on that new stuff. I spent the break down in Florida with my cousin and 'nem. They put me on these shrooms," Highlighter pulled out a sandwich bag full of mushrooms.

"Oh, wow, you've upgraded from school supplies." I couldn't help but smile at the thought of Highlighter's latest phase.

"Ay, laugh all you want, but if you nibble on some of these bad boys, you'll be flying for weeks," Highlighter explained.

"I told you. I'm good," I said while wiping tears from my eyes.

"Yea, okay. Well, take these just in case. You're too pretty to be out here snapping on lockers." Highlighter smiled before dropping the mushrooms into my book bag and walking off.

I looked closely at the contents of the sandwich bag. I couldn't believe Highlighter was eating fungi for a drug high. I giggled one last time before throwing them back into my book bag and heading off to find my first class.

The faint smell of chemicals made it clear that I was starting my morning off with Chemistry. I hated Chemistry. It was as if some idiot decided to combine math and science in the worst way possible just to torture high school kids. As if the subject itself wasn't bad enough, I walked in just in time to see the Lix sitting in the front row of class. I almost wanted to regurgitate at the sight of their smug expressions.

"I could've sworn we were in Chemistry and not Biology, so what's the species of this specimen? I've never seen an animal with nappier fur," Rima said.

"No, you were right. This is Chemistry, so you girls should be careful sucking on those lollipops around all these chemicals. God forbid either of you happens to sprout a third face." I returned her jab with an equal level of sarcasm.

They all rolled their eyes with disgust as I walked pass them. It felt good to silence those three witches, and it seemed I wasn't alone in my moment of satisfaction. A girl I had never seen before, sitting on the back row, shined with happiness at the sight of the Lix's repulsion.

"Hey, your name's Rumor right?" the girl said while waving in my direction. She didn't look like anyone I had ever seen in Mississippi. She was different in an exotic way. Shoulder length, golden dreadlocks hung from her head. Her locks were a perfect match to her peanut butter colored skin tone, but it was the shiny ring that pierced her nose that intrigued me the most.

"Yeah, that's me. I'm sorry but I can't remember if we've met," I said.

"We've never met. Today is actually my first day. My family just moved here from New York City about a week ago. I'm Kayla." Her smile widened as if she'd just met her idol.

"Nice to meet you Kayla, but how do you know my name?" I asked.

"Girl, you are so humble. Everybody knows about Rumor Arden. Girl you took down a legend. Everybody knows about V. Gatto in New York," Kayla explained.

"Oh, I should've known. I don't really wanna think about any of that right now," I said while turning to find an empty seat.

"I'm sorry. I won't bring it up again. You should sit here with me. We can be lab partners," said Kayla.

"You're new. You don't know how things work around here. Most girls in this school hate me. Do yourself a favor and hop on that bandwagon."

"Take a good look at me, Miss Rumor. Do I look like someone who rides bandwagons?" As she spoke the sunlight shone through the window and glistened against her nose ring. She confidently through her head backwards. Her golden dreads slapped against her shoulders. She was right. There were clearly no bandwagons in Mississippi for a girl like her.

"You know what? I think I will take this seat lab partner," I said as I sat down next to her.

"Good morning, class. Take out your textbooks and turn to the Periodic Table in your indexes. Today we'll be studying the Alkali Metals." Class commenced as Mr. Hawthorne taught from his projector.

I have to admit that I didn't learn a thing about the Periodic Table or Alkali Metals that day. The morning hours passed quickly as Kayla and I quickly became acquainted. We talked until our teachers couldn't take it anymore. But even after several lectures, we passed notes back and forth as if we were carrier pigeons. By the way we chatted; you'd think we were lifelong friends.

Later in the lunch room, the Lix were infuriated by the sight of Kayla and me bonding. They barely even touched their plates while glaring across the cafeteria in our direction. Kayla took notice of the unwarranted attention, and decided to give them a show. She threw her head back and laughed loudly as if I was some sort of comedienne. Rima gagged. I enjoyed seeing the three of them boil over with hatred. It was the perfect redemption.

"I think I'm going to love having you around. I haven't seen those three this uncomfortable since the day a rat escaped from the Biology lab," I said while grinning like the Cheshire Cat.

"Girl, I've been dealing with jealous chicks all of my life. Those three are like pie compared to some of the heifers in New York." As Kayla spoke, she couldn't help but glance through her peripheral vision at the sight of an approaching Tahiri.

"Damn Rumor, I'm a little late and you got this Medusa looking chick sitting in my seat." Tami sneered while slamming her lunch tray on the table in front of Kayla.

"Tami, be cool. She's nice. This is Kayla," I explained.

"I don't care if the broad's name is weasel. Why is she sitting in my spot? You know we don't deal with these fraudulent chicks in Hurley," said Tami.

"She's not from Hurley. She's a New York City girl. She and her family just moved here a week ago," I said.

"Oh, really? Thick ass dookie braids must be all the rage in New Yitty." Tami joked while lifting one of Kayla's locks with her finger. "Besides, who is her family, anyway? I ain't heard nothing about any newbies."

"Not cool, Tami," I said through clenched teeth.

"It's okay, Rumor. I wouldn't expect your friend to know anything about dread locks or the natural movement," said Kayla while scooting down to make room for Tami. She didn't even acknowledge Tami's question about her family.

"Please do explain, honey. What big city fool convinced you that those old Harriet Tubman naps are cute?" Tami sat down without once removing Kayla from her stare.

"Like I said, it's called the natural movement. It's too many sistas out here poisoning themselves with chemicals to fit some European ideal of what our hair should look like, so you're damn right I'm rocking my Harriet Tubman naps. I'm a free rider, and ain't no shame in my game sweetie." Kayla spoke with a level of courage that not many could muster in a war of words against a Tahiri.

"Okay girl, I hear ya. Just don't be pushing me to cut off my long and lovely, because I loves me some creamy crack." As tough as Tami was, I think she enjoyed Kayla's spunk.

"No worries, girlfriend. The big chop is not for everybody," Kayla said.

"The big chop?" I asked.

"Yeah, that's what we chemical free girls call it when our natural cherries are popped. You cut away all of your processed hair and allow your nappy roots to grow free," Kayla explained.

"Rumor, don't be sitting here listening to this Negro National Nappism. You better perm them roots before your hair tries to run from your head like your lil' friend's here. I mean look at her, her hair's been kinky for so long, it's sprouting lil' golden legs," Tami teased.

"I think it's cool, Kayla. Your hair is beautiful to me," I said.

"So is yours. It's way too beautiful to be hiding behind that head-band. You should set it free," said Kayla.

"Girl, I wish. I can't pull off the whole natural thing," I sighed.

"Rumor, you are a beautiful, black woman. There is no hair that could ever define you." Kayla's words were way too similar to words that I heard from my own mother all those years before.

"Oh my God, Rumor where'd you get this?" Tami's excitement yanked me away from my recollections. She had reached into my book bag and pulled out the sandwich bag full of mushrooms.

"Put those down. Why are you going through my bag?" I exclaimed.

"Oh, those look fresh too. I haven't seen a good bag of shrooms in years." Kayla's face lit up at the sight of the drugs.

"See, Rumor, your new friend wants to try them. You can't be rude. Show this girl your southern hospitality," said Tami.

"You're going to get us put out of school. Put those away." My nerves were on edge as Tami waved the bag in the air. Our school's principal, Mr. Cheadle, was only feet away from our table.

"Girl, please. Principal Cheadle is as blind as a fruit bat," said Tami.

"We've got ten minutes before lunch is over. I say we try out those shrooms on the other side of school in the janitor's closet," sugagested Kayla.

"Two to one says you're outnumbered, Rumor." Tami winked with mischief.

I couldn't believe that I actually allowed them to talk me into it, but it wasn't long before the three of us sat inside a tiny closet inhaling a haze of mushrooms and smoke. Tami was already feeling good. Her eyes were low, her head bobbed back and forth, but no music was playing. I held my breath with all of my might while trying not to inhale the mushrooms. Kayla held the fat joint in her hand, packed tight with burning mushrooms.

"Close your eyes, Rumor. Legend has it that the herbs of the Earth can usher one's soul to the spirit realm. Feel the high." As Kayla spoke, I complied by shutting my eyes. I could feel her close to me as she exhaled smoke in my face. I took one large breath, pulling in her warm smoke. Intense sensations pulsated throughout my body. It felt as if my nerves were tiny spiders crawling beneath my skin. My head felt like a hot air balloon, carrying my body across smoky clouds.

A nearly solid haze of smoke filled the closet. Tami and Kayla both vanished as a scene of fumes blocked them from my view. It wasn't long before I was left alone with my high induced thoughts. The voices of the mushrooms sang in my head. They were calling my name with melodic scales, each one of their voices slightly more piercing than the last. I tried to grip my floating head, but by then it was too light to contain. The mushrooms were now commanding me, and I had no choice but to follow their every beck and call.

With my hand stretched out to lead the way, I stepped deeper into the smoke. I felt as if I were sleep-walking. The small janitor's closet expanded into a world beyond belief. The smoke dissipated to reveal a large bar in what appeared to be a 1920's speakeasy. It was like watching one of those old AMC movies that Aunt HoneyBea loved, except for the fact that every face in the bar was one that I had seen before. Sitting on a dozen bar stools lining the edge of the bar were random citizens of Hurley. Our mail guy was taking shots with Sheriff Mack, and Sister Mary Gibson seductively sipped on a cocktail while eyeing the butcher from the produce market as he gouged on salty peanuts. It was strange to see people who had hardly ever interacted conversing as if they were the best of buddies.

Members of my family all sat across the floor on scattered tables. As I walked past them, they continued to drink and talk as if I was invisible. I waved my hands before Aunt HoneyBea's face as she and Sister Emmagene laughed the night away, but neither of them reacted. While sitting at another table, Uncle Champ leaned back against his chair. Each time he laughed, his jiggling belly shook the table. On the other end of the table, Darryl Junior sat with his arms wide while expressively telling what seemed to be a very amusing story. I even slammed my hand against their table, but Darryl Junior's story continued as if I didn't exist.

Only a few feet away, the stage glowed with the light of a concentrated spotlight. A trail of sequined sparkles flowed across blue fabric as the most beautiful gown came into view. Standing before the dress was a microphone stand that extended upwards into an oblong microphone. Candy red lips pouted over the microphone before a honey-voiced musical note, which could only be described as the song of a sensual siren, sung beautifully. As I took in the full view of the singing vixen, it became obvious that I was staring at the image of my cousin, Gia. I couldn't believe what I was hearing. I'd heard Gia's shower singing, and her voice sounded more like a dying, rabid cat than a sexy siren. Those mushrooms had to have been doing some serious work on me.

I shook my head hoping to wake from my delirium, but as I opened my eyes, the only thing that changed was the sudden appearance of a tailored-suit wearing, fedora sporting D. There was a sparkle in his eyes that made his tight-eyed glare even more alluring than I remembered. He tipped the rim of his fedora in my direction before turning to disappear behind a hidden door adjacent to the bar. I quickly followed him down a long, dark corridor.

At the end of the passageway, was a spacious room with glass walls. We had traveled down beneath the speakeasy, but the room was strangely surrounded with dark clouds. A hint of orange sunlight touched the top of the clouds. The setting sun created walls of blue, black and orange skies. It was a beautiful, but at the same time ominous sight made complicated by the presence of a not so distant enemy.

"It is my pleasure to see you again, dear Rumor. It's not often that the devil gets to dance with her successor." Facing the backdrop of complex clouds was none other than Vendetta Gatto.

"Okay, I know I'm trippin'. What the hell are you doing in my dreams?" I slowly stepped backwards out of fear of the woman who had caused my family so much pain. She looked similar to the way I remembered her, only younger and a lot more healthy. She was tall with the lean muscular figure of an amazon. The skin of her face was tightly stretched across her high cheekbones, long jaw line, and Siamese cat eyes. Her presence rivaled the intimidation of a lion pride. As I slowly tried to escape her, I was quickly cut off by D. who stood behind me.

"No more running, Angel Eyes. It's time to start living," said D. while blocking the doorway with his amazing stature.

"Come closer, child. Let Mama Cat get a good look at you," said V. Gatto.

"I don't believe this. Lula Mae?" I asked, still puzzled by her presence.

"Please, Rumor. Call me V. I think we've moved past the point of unfamiliar aliases."

"What is the point of this? What do you want with me?" I asked.

"I can't blame you for your hesitation. I lived my life as a fool to reject you. I never saw the value in my son or his weakness for your mother, but the greatest benefit of the afterlife seems to be the omniscient perspective. You are a strong child, much stronger than I ever was at your age. It's time that you accept the mantle. It's time for mama's kitten to become mama cat." V. Gatto stood before me with eye contact so strong that I could feel her staring into my soul. She inhaled so deeply from her cigarette holder that she exhaled all of my frightened soul with her next breath.

"You took my mother away from me, drove my father insane, and literally brought all kinds of hell on Hurley, and you have the audacity to believe that I'd ever carry your mantle. I hope they have head doctors in hell because you're out of your mind," I said with all the venom I could muster.

"I've done wrong by you, but my inheritance is yours. All I ask is that you claim it. Do what you want with it. You can undo all of my wrongs if you choose to, but I have a feeling that there is more to you than what meets the eye."

"Yeah, and all of it hates you."

"Honey, the line between hate and admiration couldn't be thinner. At the end of the day, it's all love," she said while flashing a smile that made me cringe.

"The day you died was a great day for me. If I could have, I would've danced all across your grave." I said, with a mixture of venom and joy.

"Then answer this for me, kitten. Why have you held on to my black diamond?" said Gatto as a haze of smoke flowed from her mouth. The smoke was so thick that it temporarily blinded me before ushering me back into reality.

"As you can see Mister...I'm sorry I don't think I have your name." Before the smoke cleared, Principal Cheadle's banter broke through the barriers of my dream.

"Call me D.," His voice left me with chills. He and Principal Cheadle were quickly approaching me. I couldn't tell whether it was fright or excitement, but I felt an urgency to get as far away from him as possible. I was no longer in the janitor's closet with Tami and Kayla. Somehow the mushrooms had left me stranded in the middle of the hallway.

"Just D., no last name or other letters? Interesting," Principal Cheadle continued.

"Yup, Just D."

"Well, D., I have to say I was expecting to see Champ himself for a project this extreme. We have about 10 busses with engine problems."

"Mr. Champ knows I can handle it. Just show me the busses." There was a level of firmness in D's voice that made it clear he was becoming annoyed with Principal Cheadle.

"Yes, of course. They are just around this corner..." before Principal Cheadle could complete his directions, he and I met with a head-on collision. Confused by a combination of panic and mushrooms, my attempt to flee was doomed by the fact that I'd ran in the wrong direction.

"What in the world has gotten into you, Rumor?" Principal Cheadle yelled.

"Damn, girl, slow down." Tami came running from around the corner and stopped dead in her tracks at the sight of Principal Cheadle and I on the floor.

"You two reek of smoke. Get to my office now. I'm expelling you both," said Principal Cheadle as he struggled to his feet.

"Oh c'mon, Cheadle. Chill out," said Tami.

"It's Principal Cheadle to you, little girl," said Principal Cheadle enraged.

"Mr. Cheadle, don't you think suspension is a bit much. They're teenagers. They're supposed to experiment with illegal substances," said D. while aiding me to my feet. The effects of the mushrooms were still blazing through my blood stream, which heightened my senses. The feel of D.'s rough, warm, and sweaty palm caused my heart rate to jump through the roof.

"Mr. D., I won't tell you how to change motor oil if you don't tell me how to manage my school," Principal Cheadle yelled.

"Okay, Alex. I tried to do this the easy way." D.'s eyes displayed the appealing glimmer from my dream.

"How do you know my first name?" Principal Cheadle asked.

"You're Alex Jermaine Cheadle. You live on 1515 Chestnut Drive and I'm sure the parents of Hurley, Mississippi would love to know how you spend your weekends away from managing their children. Small town families don't exactly have a reputation for being open-minded," said D. whispering just loud enough for Principal Cheadle and me to understand him.

"I don't know what the hell you are talking about!" Mr. Cheadle tried to play stupid, but by the look on his face he knew exactly what D. was speaking of. "This time I'll overlook this little infraction, but you girls need to wash the smell of smoke from yourselves and get back to class."

"I'm glad we have an understanding." D. smirked as Principal Cheadle hastily walked away.

"This makes the second time you've saved our asses. I don't know about you girl, but I'd love another scoop of chocolate guardian angel on my plate," said Tami flirting.

"You okay, Angel Eyes?" D.'s deep baritone voice sent my drug-fueled hormones into overdrive.

Before I could contain myself, I pulled him into a close embrace. He did not relent. His warm breath blew across my lips causing them to tingle slightly. My lips quivered as half of me feared the mysterious man, but the other half desired him more than anything. I grabbed his face forcefully, pulling his lips into mine. The skin of our lips was soft and wet as my tingling was soon calmed by the impact. We both pulled away slightly to take in the look of the other's eyes. Almost like magnets, our pupils pulled us closer. Passion caused my lips to part as his tongue entered my mouth. It was a feeling I had never felt before. I was surprised until my tongue found the rhythm of his mouth. Our lips smacked as our tongues danced against one another. It was warm and sensual. All time stopped as we melted into a moment of pure ecstasy.

Mesmerized by the spell of D.'s tongue, I slowly backed out of his embrace. I held my fingers firmly against my lips as if I feared losing the after-effects of his kiss. I then twisted my mouth into a confident sneer, yanked the headband from my hair, and turned to wink at Tami.

"Girl, what has gotten into you? Cause I like it!" Tami exclaimed before we both ran off giggling down the hallway.

Later as I stood before the school's bathroom mirror looking at my exposed nappy hairs, I felt free. I felt freer than I have ever felt before. I'd taken my first steps into the wild side, and it was more enticing than I would have ever imagined. I wanted more.

"She kissed him?" Kayla asked as she and Tami laughed at my exploits.

"Girl, it was all sloppy and wet like they were trying to eat each other's faces off. Ah, it was so hot," said Tami.

"Rumor, you are amazing girl." Kayla laughed.

"Rumor, why are you so quiet?" Tami's tone grew more serious as they both shot concerned looks in my direction.

I stood facing the mirror with my hair pulled into a ponytail. I removed a pair of scissors from my book bag and held them close to my hair. "So what do you think, Kayla? Am I ready for the big chop?"

"Stop playing and put those scissors down," Tami ordered. But she was too late as the blades of the scissors quickly cut through my hair. I rubbed my fingers through the unkempt afro that was left and smiled.

"Meow," I purred while taking in the full visual of the woman that I was becoming.

Rumor's Journal Entry 3

They say ain't nothing happy
About being nappy,
Girlfriend got all of them kinks in her hair,
It's a ratchet mess, girl, I swear.
Lookin' like a fool whose lost someone's dare.
How about you pick up a brush and act like you care?
Her head's a disgrace, nothing but tangles there,
So she pulls out her scissors, the sharpest pair,
To free her roots and display that her natural beauty is
beyond compare.

CHAPTER 5

Bad News
As Told By D

The number one rule of being a hustler is to know as much as possible about your enemy, and to me, everyone was an enemy. Even before I was ever released from prison, I dominated the streets with an iron fist. The name D. Ception was one to be feared and respected. Working the prison's auto-body shop gave me access to important city vehicles like busses, taxis, police cars, and the best luxury cars for politicians. You'd be surprised how much privileged information was usually left in those vehicles. I learned at an early age that powerful men are weakened most by the secrets they choose to keep.

I was like a machine the way I tore down the New Orleans elite with no regard for their emotions. Being incapable of love made me impervious to sentiments like compassion and regret which slowed most men down. But standing in the midst of a lot full of school busses, I realized that for the first time in my life I was in danger of losing it all.

I could still feel her lips against mine. Rumor had touched a part of me that I didn't know still existed. I couldn't stop thinking about her. I needed to execute my hustle over her, but somehow she'd found the heart inside of the monster. I couldn't help but wonder if I was hustling her or was it her who was hustling me?

The school was empty, but I stayed late, determined to make

leeway on fixing the faulty school busses. It started as a pretty peaceful night. The moon was full. Cricket chirps bounced back and forth between rows of Calico bushes. Random bursts of fresh air blew with intensity. With only a small tank top covering my chest, the wind massaged me like the cool palms of angels. The whistle of the whipping winds blew into my ears. The light airy sound reminded me of Rumor. The scent of blowing petals and pollen couldn't even compare to the natural fragrance of my Angel Eyes.

Aggravated by frustration, I flung my wrench onto the black top parking lot. I needed to call it a night. Rumor's kiss had enchanted me. No matter how hard I tried, I couldn't focus on the busses at all. I needed to get as far away from Hurley High School as possible and regain my focus on the mission ahead. There were only a few short weeks left before Rumor's 16th birthday. She would soon be a very wealthy young woman, and I needed to quickly claim my stake to her inheritance.

As I returned my tools to their proper places in my toolbox, I found myself alerted by the sound of approaching voices. It was about eight o' clock that night, and the school should have been vacant. I reopened my toolbox and removed a hammer. As a master manipulator, I'd gained a countless amount of enemies and learned to always maintain my guard.

Cordell, some cat on the school's basketball team, came strutting into the school building like a broken down boss. "Man, these broads won't know what hit them."

"I don't know about this, man. What if Coach Khaled finds out we did this?" said some chinky-eyed fool named Taylor following behind him. My ears perked with interest because the dude's name sounded way too familiar.

"Tay-Dog, stop being a pussy, man. I don't remember Coach Khaled trippin' when the girl's team knotted all of our shoe-strings together. It took us all day to untie all those shoes," said Cordell.

"True. Alright, but we need to move quickly. I'm not trying to get caught. Where is Highlighter?" Taylor's voice jumped several decibels, showing his cowardice like a new coat of chicken feathers.

"Playas don't fear, Highlighter is near." Highlighter stepped out of the shadows. There was something about that kid that I strangely respected. He had true potential for the hustle.

"What took you so long?" Cordell frowned.

"What took ya'll so long? I've been here, and with plenty of these," said Highlighter while pulling jars of tomato paste from a duffel bag.

"You see? What did I tell you, Tay-Dog? Highlighter always comes through with the product," Cordell bragged while taking in the sight of the jars.

I quietly stalked in the background as the three of them proceeded to the girls' basketball team's locker room. Interestingly enough, they had a toolbox of their own. I tightened my grip on my own hammer just in case they discovered me.

"Ay, take this wrench and remove the shower heads. This is gonna be classic," said Cordell while rubbing his hands together in a boastful manner.

"Why do I have to screw off the shower heads? What about your boy, Highlighter?" Taylor complained.

"I'm just here for the supply, homie," said Highlighter with a container of Elmer's glue pressed against his nostrils.

"Dude, you need help." Taylor shot Highlighter a look of disapproval.

"Why don't you just pretend those shower heads are Rima and Rumor? You never had any problems screwing either of them," Highlighter jibbed back at Taylor. That's when I realized why the fool's name was so familiar to me. Taylor was the punk that Rumor was upset about the night that I met her.

"How about you mind your damn business?" Taylor charged

at Highlighter, but Cordell immediately jumped in-between the two of them.

"Ya'll acting like some girls, man. Just take off the damn shower heads. I'll fill them with the sauce. I'm not trying to hear all this drama. I just wanna see naked chicks running down the hallway with jiggling, red titties," said Cordell.

"Whatever, man. I just need some fresh air real quick. The smell of glue is starting to make me sick," Taylor stormed out of the locker room, roughly pushing past Highlighter with his right shoulder.

"Yo, what's wrong with your boy? I was just making a lil' joke," asked Highlighter.

"Well clown, pick up that wrench because you just joked your way into unscrewing those shower heads," barked Cordell.

Meanwhile on the outside of the school, Taylor frantically marched back and forth. He groaned loudly while complaining to himself. "What the hell is wrong with females these days? I mean what did I do that's so wrong? Rumor's supposed to be here for me, but instead she's giving me the damn cold shoulder for absolutely no reason at all. I just wish I knew what was going on. I know Rima's pregnant, but Rumor and I are just friends. That's all we've ever been, right? She does know me better than anyone else on this planet. We sit up and laugh all day about the dumbest things. I miss her so much. What does this mean? God, please help me figure out what is going on with my life."

Listening to Taylor ramble on about his problems sickened me. It was bad enough that Rumor cared so much about the punk, but even worse it was beginning to sound like he had feelings for her as well. I could see that he was going to be that one annoying pawn blocking me from taking my queen. Nothing or no one ever came in between me and my prey. I cracked my knuckles while tightening my glare with homicidal determination. Taylor was my target, and I was locked, loaded and ready to fire.

I could tell by the way he stood suspiciously still that he could feel danger creeping towards him. The pit of his stomach must have felt like a cesspool of slithering nerves because I could see him trembling as he turned to face me. The further I stepped beyond the evening shadows, the more his eyes widened. I loved feeding from the fear of my victims. As I approached Taylor, he smelled like a tasty topping of terror.

"Is this some kind of prank? Let me guess, Cordell sent you to scare me for not helping unscrew those shower heads. Well whoever you are, you can go tell him that it's not working." By the way that his voice shook, it was clear that Taylor didn't even believe his own declaration of courage.

"I don't know why I'm so surprised to see the piece of a man standing in front of me. Now that I think about it, what kind of man is a best friend to a woman?" I said.

"Look man, I don't know who you are, and you damn sure don't know the first thing about me." Taylor attempted to force his way past me, but I gripped his arm with a force equal to that of a pit bull's bite. His adrenaline must've kicked in because he turned to pull away from me, but my grip did not ease. We both locked eyes with dangerously intimidating stares.

"Let me tell you something, pretty boy. This ain't some movie where the good guy finds his happy ending. This look in my eyes means bad news. I could snap your neck right now without even losing a drop of sweat." The more intense my mug became, the more Taylor's softened. I knew his whole bad boy front wouldn't hold up, because staring into my eyes is like looking down the barrel of a fully loaded machine gun.

"I don't want any problems. I was just leaving. Okay?" Taylor's voice trembled as the anxiety of his predicament set in.

With one swift move, I threw him into a chokehold. I could feel his nervous sweat dripping onto my arm. I found pleasure in his whimpering as he fully succumbed to my control. Taylor was the type of kid that wouldn't make it a day in the juvenile system. I'd seen so many like him. They always ended up either dead or someone's prison trick.

"C'mon man. Just let me go," Taylor begged.

"Sssh. Calm down before you piss yourself. If I wanted you dead, you'd be dead already. You see there's an artery in your neck that runs straight to your brain. With the push of one finger, I could shut down the blood flow and put you to sleep permanently," I said.

"Please, man. Just let me go." Taylor continued to plead for his life.

"Go home to your mommy, sweetness. If you know what's good for you, you'll stay away from Rumor. She's my girl now, and I can be dangerously possessive." I spoke slowly with Deep breaths against his ear. I then flexed my arm, tightening my grip on his throat. He gagged for a while. Just as I could feel the life draining from his body, I left a kiss on his cheek, a warning move I usually gave to those who even looked as if they wanted to try me while in lock up. Once I was sure the message had been received, I released him to the ground where he held his aching throat and panted for oxygen.

"Ay man, back the hell up off my boy." Cordell stepped out to the parking lot just in time to see me standing over a kneeling Taylor.

"Lucky me, I get to have more fun." I smiled, but before I could even turn to take a look at Cordell, the parking lot was filled with piercing bright beaming headlights. There were many of them coming from all directions. We were surrounded. In the tussle with Taylor, I had not even heard the engines of what appeared to be black SUVs.

"Taylor, are you okay?" Cordell rushed out to help Taylor up on his feet. Highlighter soon came running out as well. I paid the three of them little attention as I remained focused on the bright lights of the surrounding vehicles.

The car doors opened. It all seemed to happen in slow motion as armed men appeared from behind the tinted glass of the car doors. I had to think quickly. I couldn't risk being exposed by the attention that would come with the blood shed of innocent high school boys, so I knew that I had to protect them. I stood at the center of the spotlight created by the beaming headlights. I slowly raised my hands into the air, making it clear that I was surrendering.

"Man, I must be high as spit because it looks like the mother-ship just landed dead smack onto Hurley High school." Highlighter stood wide eyed and amazed. Taylor and Cordell, on the other hand, both used their arms to shield their eyes from all of the light.

"Get your dumb asses out of here," I yelled at the three of them while maintaining my stance in the center of the circle of SUVs.

"You heard the man. Get out of here now." The largest of the armed men stepped into the light signaling for the boys to leave. Cordell, Highlighter and Taylor wasted no time escaping the school's grounds.

It wasn't long before I realized that I'd seen the man before. His massive frame immediately gave him away. He was the same clown who snuck me when I met my last black market client.

"Coming back for round two, I see," I said with both fists clenched.

"Look around you, D. The numbers aren't in your favor, so let's make this as easy as possible," he said while removing a pair of shades that revealed the bruises I'd left on his face.

"Didn't they teach you how to spell? There are no D.'s in the word easy, but you will end with one when things get hard." Even in the focus of blindingly bright light, I moved like lightening. The fool was so foolishly confident in the company of his armed friends that he didn't even see it coming. I pulled the gun from his grasp and slammed him face first against the asphalt with my knee plunging into his back. The gun, now in my hand, was directly aimed for his bald head.

"You're being stupid, D. If you don't cooperate, there's no way you're going to make it out of this one alive." The man struggled to speak with half his mouth lying on the ground.

"All I have to do is wait. You just sent three witnesses running into the night. You best believe this place will be crawling with cops soon." I smiled.

"Shoot him!" the man shouted.

Several rounds of pistol fire blasted in our direction, but I used his body as a shield to block the bullets. The ammunition ate away at the large man's body long enough for me to find my way back inside the school building. With the one gun in hand, I fled down the hallways of the school. I could tell the men had been instructed to keep things low-key because they were careful not to fire any bullets inside of the school. Most of their cars had sped off after the brief shoot out, but I could still hear the foot-steps of the ones who had been left behind. They weren't far behind me. I listened closely to their steps. There were four of them. However, unbeknownst to them, four was my lucky number.

They eventually tracked me down to the cafeteria kitchen. I stooped low behind a large tray rack. I could hear them as they carefully searched throughout each corner. While peering over bread trays, I watched the four of them. There was a short, chubby one; I called him Stumpy. Another guy with a beard as thick as lion fur checked the school's giant freezer for signs of my whereabouts. I gave him the name, Simba. I also noticed some bug-eyed fool who I was surprised couldn't see me through the steel rack. I'll call him Maggot. Then the last one was a very serious looking Asian dude. By the way he directed their search I could tell that he was in charge. I think I called him Emperor.

After I fully scoped them out, I was ready to dance. Stumpy was the first to advance. I felt him peering around the right side of the tray. His little, stubby fingers appeared from between the racks providing me the signal to act. I smashed his unsuspecting face with a tray of bread. As the tray vibrated from its collision with Stumpy's face, Maggot rushed me. We both fell backwards on a cold food table. I held onto the sneeze guard and after a double leg lift, kicked Maggot across the room.

With two chopping knives in his hands, Simba slashed against thin air while walking toward me. The speed of the two blades in his hands caused the most threatening whipping sound. From the other side, Emperor stood in a battle ready stance. My eyes shot back and forth between the two of them as my mind devised my next move. I threw the organizer full of condiment packages at Simba. He slashed through them, causing ketchup, mustard, and mayonnaise to squirt into his eyes. With Simba temporarily blinded by condiments, I grabbed his wrists to prevent him from wielding the chopping knives. I then drove my elbow into his face. I wasn't sure whether I was seeing ketchup or his blood as I threw him into Emperor.

Emperor was fast. He dodged Simba effortlessly. All I could do was shield my face as Emperor rained down on me with a combination of punch attacks. He was more skilled than the other three. I blocked him with my forearms as long as I could, but Emperor's punches were strong. His fist broke through my block. My face was on fire beneath the impact of his knuckles. My mouth filled with blood as his left and right fists used my face as a punching bag. Delirious from Emperor's tirade of attacks, I struggled to maintain my stance. He stood about a foot away from me before his high kick sent me flying backwards. My head landed with a thud against the ground causing me to completely black out. I had fallen into the downside of any hustle. It's only so long anyone can manipulate the streets before the streets start to clap back.

Like a mental slide show, the cold, dead eyes of my crack addicted mother raced through my mind. She appeared to be a walking corpse the way she would silently saunter throughout our studio apartment. There were many nights that I would have to drag her unconscious body from the filthy hallways of our project apartment building. She stunk of alcohol, urine, regurgitation, and unsafe sex. Even at six years old, I knew that she was a dead woman walking. She barely ever spoke to me unless it was to curse the day that I was born. I hated her for being so weak. My resentment for her filled my vision with the blood-red stain of my fury. All I could see was red, and it intensified until there was nothing left but blood. My entire life had been nothing but multiple incidents of spilled blood, and it had all started with my mother.

"Wake the hell up!" More blood splattered from my mouth as a man's alligator-skinned dress shoe smashed into my rib cage. Even in a state of delirium, I knew the voice that was speaking to me. It was my client.

I didn't get a good look at him when we met in New Orleans, but his creepy laughter was exactly the same. It gave me chills. It was all too similar to the disturbing noises that my mother would make as I drug her nearly dead body from the cold hallway of our apartment building. She would struggle for each breath, gasping for a life that she had long ago lost. The man's kicks to my abdomen were nothing compared to the torture of hearing his incessant laughter.

"Well slap my belly and call me Sally. I'm in the big leagues now. Ain't too many men can brag about shining their Gators with the blood of the south's biggest goon." The man continued to laugh.

"I'm glad you got your rocks off. Now do you wanna let me up from here?" I yanked against the ropes that were binding my wrists and ankles.

"Sorry bud, but I really can't do that. Don't get me wrong though. It's not personal. I'm a fan. I really am. But I just can't allow you to make me out to be a punk in these streets. You know how it is," he explained through a very thick southern accent. He must've masked it the first time we spoke, because I didn't remember it being so pronounced.

"Okay look, I know I'm supposed to be instigating a war for you in New Orleans, but we ran into a little snag on that plan. Everything is still under control," I said.

"I'm assuming they don't have Direct TV down here in the boonies, because the national headlines seem to think that you don't have it under control," he yelled as if I were a thief on the run with his money. His entire demeanor changed as the creepy laughter finally stopped. His face froze into a hard look of displeasure.

"National headlines?" I asked.

"Some pig ass cop fella who goes by the name of Mack has the police and protestors holding hands while singing old Negro hymns. How am I supposed to sell my ammunition if everybody's all hunky dory?" he continued to explain. The thick lines in his forehead scrunched together like the wires of a slinky. He snarled through his wide nose, giving the appearance of an overgrown pig. He was a very bright-skinned man. I assumed he was black but most likely mixed with some other race, possibly Italian or Spanish. As round as his face appeared, his tailored suit framed a large body that appeared to be well maintained.

"Damn, I should've known that over-achieving rookie would mess everything up," I said.

"It seems we've gotten off to a bad start here, Mr.C`eption.

101

Before I tried the whole bourgeois and mysterious approach, but clearly that doesn't work well with you street coons, so look me in my face. I'm Nefarius Grimm, and I can be your best friend or your worst nightmare; that's your choice. What I will not be is played by some 18-year-old delinquent, who has manipulated the world into thinking that he is some kind of street king."

"I'm not trying to play you," I urged.

"I already know that, bud. You see I had to do a little research of my own. You don't get to my level by not knowing what's going on with your hired help. It looks like you've stumbled on a very big treasure, a Gatto-sized treasured. I want a piece of that."

"That's not the job you hired me for."

"While you're working for me, everything that you do is what I hired you to do. You will finish both hustles. I want my war and half of the lovely Gatto's money. If I don't get both by the time your little southern princess turns sixteen, I'll kill both you and her."

"You think I give a damn about her?" I lied.

"You can fool some people some of the time, but you can't fool all of us every time. Like I said, I've been doing my research. I know about your little kiss with the girl. I believe her name is Rumor. I will kill her, D., so please don't try and play me."

"You claim to be a fan of my work, right? Do you really think threatening me is going to get you what you want?" By then, I was enraged by his desired claim to my hustle.

"Let me show you how sure I am in my belief that until you finish both jobs you belong to me." Nefarius once again pressed play on his creepy laughter. I watched as he stood directly above me and unzipped his designer pants. My eyes bucked widely as he pulled out his penis and proceeded to urinate on me. His hot piss felt like acid as it burned every inch of me. I pulled against the ropes that were binding me with all of my strength. I wanted to rip his larynx from his fat throat.

"You've been marked; 'Property of Nefarius,'" he said as the sole of his size 13 shoe stomped down upon my face. Once again, I had fallen to the bitter darkness of defeat.

D's Journal Entry 2

Every man has a hustle Deep within his soul;
A competition against the devil for complete control.
Like a man reading a story that's still untold,
The purpose is the part that he can't unfold.
He stands tall with ill intention; lost but bold,
So all he'll ever know is defeat; both dark and cold.

CHAPTER 6

Wounded Pride
As Told by D

The next morning as I returned to the school-yard, it was clear that Nefarius had no plans of cutting me any kind of slack. In every direction I turned, I saw a flunky with a suit. To all the school's faculty and students, Nefarius's goons blended in like the rest of the alumni. They moved with complete discretion as they made their way through the school building in anticipation of the annual Homecoming Pep Rally, but it was nothing for me to detect the presence of a fellow criminal. I could see their shifty eyes and bruised knuckles from a mile away. The monster in me wanted revenge. I wanted to stand and watch as Nefarius and all of his men burned like the tarred embers of a wild-fire, but I decided to play it safe instead. I would give him the impression that I was playing along with his plans just long enough to switch the tide in my favor.

In the meantime I would not forget the bruising and pain that I awoke to the previous night. The smell of Nefarius's rancid piss became the least of my worries as I found myself lying face first in a pile of dog feces. I was still shuttering at the thought of the fresh turd oozing from my face. A warning growl from an angry dog was enough to make me jump to attention. As I looked up, I was staring into the slobbering grill of a hungry Rottweiler. I was careful not to make any sudden movements, but there was nothing that I could do to calm the dog's fury. He stretched into an attack stance before barking twice. With each bark, I could see his carnivorous teeth. They were like tiny daggers as the moon light reflected from their sharp edges. I was frozen stiff as me and the dog continued to stand off in a battle of intimidation. I was determined not to let him smell an ounce of fear, that is, until two pairs of glowing eyes reached out from the night's shadows.

Not only did the barking increase, but the Rottweiler's did not hesitate to attack. I turned and ran with the dogs in full pursuit of me. I could feel the pressure from their bites snapping for my legs. With blood still dripping from my face, I was primed for their devouring. I was sure they were going to tear me apart until I climbed over a nearby hill to see a high metal fence. I delved for the fence, reaching as high as I possibly could. As I finally gripped it with my body pressed firmly against the bars, the dogs were still beneath me, leaping and biting for my feet. Frantically I pulled myself to the top of the fence and flipped over it onto safe ground.

As my trembling legs touched the ground, a strike of bright lightning accompanied by loud thunder ushered in the evening rain. Blood and rain water dripped down my eyelashes. I wiped my eyes to take one last look at the iron fence. The dogs all growled and barked while standing against the backside of metal words decorated into the fence's exterior. It was the first time I had noticed them. The words read, "Johnson Manor."

Rumor was the last surviving member of the Johnson family, and because of me, she had become Nefarius' target. She seemed carefree as I watched her chat away with friends. She had no idea of the fortune that was within her grasp or of the threats that were determined to keep her from it.

"He has been staring at you since the moment we stepped into this gym," Kayla gushed. But little did she know that I was an expert lip reader.

"Mmm Hmm, look at him over there looking like a triple chocolate muscle cake." Tami shot me a set of flirty eyes that I tried my best to ignore. They were sitting in the midst of a set of bleachers across the court from where I stood.

"Tami, you are crazy. I don't know the first thing about that man," said Rumor while trying not to look in my direction. But her eyes were like magnets as they gravitated toward me.

"Girl, word on the street is that he's a Caribbean prince or something. They say he came to Hurley to find his queen." Tami's joke almost made me giggle. I know girls are into fairytales, but it's laughable to think that I could be anyone's prince.

"You really need to stop gossiping with those crack-heads in Mercy Projects." Rumor shook her head at the foolishness of Tami's story.

"If you don't want him, then say the word. I'll take him off your hands. I always did have a soft spot for chocolate," said Tami. But Rumor's focus shifted to three girls who slowly pranced in their direction.

"I'm so happy to see you girls sitting on the front row waiting for the next Lix show. We promise not to disappoint." Rima stood facing Rumor.

"Rima, even though I can see that your face is dying for a good fist bump, I'm really not in the mood to be undoing all that good work your surgeon did on your nose." Tami immediately stood to face Rima.

"Ugh, she is so ghetto," Candace snarled.

"Well, that's my cue. It's hoe draggin' time." Tami raised her hand, but Rumor stood to stop her.

"She's not worth it, girl. Besides the only way we're going to shut her up is to hit her where it hurts the most," said Rumor.

"Really? Where is that?" said Rima.

"Your pride or should I say, school pride. We're entering the pep squad competition." Rumor smirked.

"We're doing what?" Kayla interjected.

"Girl, I ain't doing that. That stuff is for lames," said Tami.

"You hear that, Lix. It sounds like we've scared a Tahiri," said Rima as she and the other two Lix laughed simultaneously.

"Scared? You may want to tighten the straps on your push-up bra, boo boo, because this road is about to get very bumpy for you. We're in," said Tami.

"See you on the court, ladies," Rumor teased as Tami and Kayla both shooed the Lix away.

Rumor was growing stronger and more confident right before my very eyes. It was a thrillingly attractive sight. Her hair was shorter than the last time I'd seen her. It was like a beehive of natural curls the way it reached upwards from her face. Without it flowing down across her face, her beauty seemed even more pronounced than I remembered.

Every hint of vulnerability had disappeared from her eyes. Her glare was fiercely confident until the blast of a confetti gun left the school shouting with cheer. The pep rally commenced with loud music and the dribbling of basketballs as the boy's team rushed the court. On all sides, the team was surrounded by cheerleaders who praised their every move. Every single face in the building, but one, filled with elation. Even from the other side of the gym, I could see the tiny puddles of sorrow that were reflected through the image of Taylor on the surface of Rumor's eyes. I hated the effect that he had on her. It was in that moment that I remembered that Taylor was a barrier that I could not afford to ignore.

A gymnasium full of screaming girls was enough to give any man a headache; I was no different. From the way they were erratically shouting, you would've thought we were all first-hand witnesses to the rapture, and Taylor was Jesus Christ himself. He effortlessly slammed the basketball through the hoop and hung onto the rim as if he were doing pull-ups. After about ten seconds of basking in high school glory, Taylor's feet returned to the court. His chest swelled high with over-inflated pride. I wanted to wipe that disgusting smirk right off his face.

After the boys' basketball team finished showing off, the crowd anxiously waited for the girls' team to rush the court. Some giant hamster, the most ridiculous mascot I've ever seen, hit a quick dance spin before extending his arm to reveal the girls. But their welcome was nowhere near as exciting as that of the boys' team. You could've heard a pin drop as five varsity girls completely covered in red tomato paste angrily stepped on the court.

Cordell fell backwards with laughter. He could not contain himself as he watched their prank materialize before his eyes. "What's wrong girls? Did you wake up on the wrong side of your cycles?"

"I knew it was that hating bastard!" said the girl's team captain, Angie, while fuming with anger. Her words found her teammates as if they were ordered to attack, because the girls charged the boy's team with blood thirst in their eyes.

"Clear the damn court!" Coach Khaled shouted as both his teams attempted to pummel one another. After a brief but intense melee, both teams separated to opposite sides of the gym. If I had any say-so, that would've been the longest part of their homecoming program. It would've made my day to see big foot Angie drop-kick Taylor across the court, but the program proceeded with the spirit competition.

"Who's got that hamster pride? Shout it out, don't let it ride!" the cheerleaders all chanted repeatedly while dancing across the court. Any damper that the fight had placed on the pep rally was immediately unapparent. The students were all stomping, shouting, clapping, and cheering as the Lix descended from the bleachers onto the court.

The three of them stood in the center of the court in a triangle shaped formation. They each had their hands planted on their hips. Rima shot Rumor a quick triumphant look before clapping her hands to initiate their performance.

"Rima's got that hamster pride! Candace got that hamster pride! Natalie got that hamster pride! Beat a Lix? Homegirl, you tried." The Lix chanted while clapping and stepping in formation. They threw their heads back and forth, shaking their hair as if they were facing the wind.

After their quick routine, the cheerleaders jumped and cheered across the gym searching for a team to challenge the Lix. You could tell the girls had cemented a reputation for themselves in the school. No one dared to challenge their school spirit, but Rumor was sporting more than just a new hairstyle; she was becoming more confident with her new dare-devil attitude.

My Angel Eyes stood to her feet in the midst of the bleachers and stomped twice against the seats. Her loud stomps commanded the attention of the entire gym, "Rumors got that hamster pride! A lame Lix would be wise to hide, step to me and that's suicide! Step to me and that's suicide!" All time stopped as I gazed upon what could have only been a day-dream. She looked like a goddess as every eye in the building worshipped the sight of her. The look of fiery confidence had returned to her face.

Looking at her in that moment, I saw angelic lights illuminating her outline. I was starting to feel sensations that I had never felt before. I couldn't even describe the feelings as they were so foreign to me, but now I know that what I felt was a combination of emotions that resulted in something I never thought possible. Rumor was becoming more than just another hustle; my attraction to her was no longer about her inheritance. For Rumor Arden, I was somehow falling in love.

With an additional two stomps, Kayla shattered my day-dream with the words, "Kayla's got that hamster pride! I'll shake my hips from side to side! Oops, I think a Lix just cried!"

As soon as Kayla completed her chant, Tami stood to join them both. "Tami's got that hamster pride! Better than me? Baby girl, you lied. Time for Tahiri homicide! Owwww!"

Everyone cleared a way as the three of them chanted and stepped from the middle bleacher down to the court. The energy within the gym peaked as everyone stomped and clapped along with their chants. Their routine became more than just a competition for victory, it became a movement for everyone who had ever wanted to bring an end to the legacy of the Lix. There was horror all over Rima's face as the cheerleaders proudly announced Rumor's team as the new pep squad.

The crazy thing is that I didn't even realize I was smiling. And I'm not talking about a small smirk either, I was literally beaming from ear to ear. She had courageously beaten the untouchable. Rumor was more than just a set of pretty angel eyes, she was the soul seductress who had hustled me out of my heart.

I made my way through a horde of excited students and alumni. I was anxious to find Rumor, but as soon as she came into view, I was disappointed to see Taylor standing next to her. Fortunately, he didn't notice me, so I was just in time to overhear their conversation.

"Congratulations, Rumor," said Taylor.

"Wow, I'm surprised you're not consoling your baby's mother right now," said Rumor.

"C'mon Rumor, you're my best friend. Besides, Rima will be fine. They always win. She has enough spirit sticks for a lifetime," said Taylor.

"Well thank you, Taylor." Rumor smiled.

"So what happened to your hair?" Taylor snickered.

"I cut it. I'm natural now. You don't like it?" asked Rumor. I hated the way in which she sought his approval.

"Usually I'm a fan of longer hair, but I've never seen you glow like this. It fits you." There was a little glimmer in his eyes as he spoke. I knew that whole friendship excuse was a bunch of bull crap.

"When are we going to hang out? I miss you." Taylor embraced Rumor. It took everything for me not to slit his throat with the blade of my Swiss army knife.

"You want to hang with me?" asked Rumor sarcastically.

"Rumor, I don't understand what's going on with you these days. You just checked out on me without even telling me why. I could've sworn that you were at my house that day to make up, but you stormed out of there like a bat out of hell. What happened?"

"I don't want to get into that." Rumor nervously avoided the question.

"Well we should really talk sometime soon. I hear you've been hanging with that new guy who's fixing the school busses. Stay away from him, Rumor. That guy is into some bad stuff," Taylor tried to warn Rumor. His warning was confirmation enough for me that I had to move him closer to the top of my hit list.

"You have got to be kidding me. Is that what this is about? Are you jealous?" asked Rumor.

"Jealous of who? What do you know about that dude?" Taylor continued. But at that point, I had enough of his crying.

I moved in to purposely interrupt their conversation, so I slightly tapped Taylor's shoulder. When he turned to face me, he looked as if he'd seen a ghost.

"Rumor, I'll catch you later. Remember what we talked about, okay?" said Taylor before disappearing into the crowd.

As much as I hated Taylor, I couldn't fathom a negative emotion while standing so closely to Rumor. "So what were you two talking about?"

"Funny that you ask. We were actually talking about you." She said while raising her eye brows and tightening her cheeks into a suspicious expression.

"Really?" I acted as if I were surprised.

"Yeah, he actually made a pretty good point. He asked me what do I know about you, and if I'm honest, I don't know anything," she said.

"Well, it's all good. He's just being a good friend to you," I lied.

"So who are you, D?" asked Rumor.

"Today's your lucky day, Rumor. I'll pick you up tonight at seven for a ride on the town. I'll tell you everything that you want to know tonight, so don't be late," I said before turning and walking away. I didn't even give her a chance to protest, even though all of her body language made it crystal clear that she was feeling me.

In only a few hours, I would be sealing the deal. The game changer was that Rumor's inheritance was no longer the goal. Rumor was my new prize. I wanted her more than anything, but in order for me to win her heart, Taylor would have to be removed from the equation.

Later that day, Taylor was the only remaining player in the locker room. He had no idea how much danger he was in. I was very light on my feet. He hadn't heard me entering the locker room at all. With black latex gloves concealing my fingerprints, I was in prime stealth mode. He sat on a wooden bench in-between lockers, staring down at the cell phone in his hands. He was distracted. It wouldn't take me 10 seconds to slit his throat. As I pulled the Swiss blade from my pocket and prepared to drive it across his skin, the sound of a voice speaking from his cell phone caused me to halt.

"How the hell did you get my cell phone, kid?" an old man's voice spoke through the phone's speaker.

"You worked in the Hurley school system for 20 years, Mr. Pete. Let's just say the girl who does work study in the principal's office has a crush on me," explained Taylor.

"Got-dammit, kid. I dealt with you lil' roaches for way too

long. Can't get rid of you damn critters. What do you need?" Old Man Pete complained.

"I need you to look into this guy for me. He goes by the name of D. I've sent you his picture already." As Taylor spoke, I was infuriated. The little punk was having me tracked by some retired federal agent. I read the files on V. Gatto's case. Federal Agent James "Pete" Benson worked her case for years. I couldn't let him expose me. Rumor would never love me if she knew the truth behind my identity. It seemed Taylor's death would have to wait for now. Federal Agent Pete was my new target.

"I'm retired, kid. Leave me alone," said Old Man Pete.

"It's for Rumor, please. Do it for Alieza," Taylor begged, knowing that Alieza was Pete's soft spot.

"Alright, kid. Meet me at the docks in an hour. Come alone." Old Man Pete commanded before ending the call.

As soon as Taylor's call had ended, I rammed my elbow into the back of his head. Taylor hit the ground with a thud. He was out cold. I didn't have much time left before my date with Rumor, so I had to quickly get to the docks before Taylor was able to wake from his forced nap.

There weren't many boats left at the docks, so it wasn't hard to find the one that Old Man Pete called home. The man had obviously done a pretty good job with saving his money because it was a very nice boat. It was too bad he wouldn't be able to live in it much longer.

Inside the boat, most of the lights were off. The sound of a flushing toilet made it clear that Pete was in the restroom. I stooped low so that he wouldn't see me as he opened the restroom door.

"You know you're old when you damn near meet your maker from the smell of your own crap. Smells like somebody gutted a pig in there." Pete waved the stench of a fresh bowel movement from his face.

"I hear you got some information for me, old man." I rose from hiding just as Old Man Pete flipped the switch to turn on the lights.

116

"D. Ception. When I found it was you, I knew you'd come," said Old Man Pete.

"Well don't worry. It's not personal, so I'll make this as painless as possible," I said.

"Quit yappin', kid. Let's dance," said Old Man Pete while quickly pulling a handgun from his office desk drawer.

"My file must not be as thorough as I thought. You should've known that was the first place I would check." I smiled while holding the bullets from his gun in my hands.

"Not bad," the old man grunted.

He pulled a walking cane from the corner and charged me. I have to admit that he was quick for an old man. I blocked my face with both arms as he swung the cane in my direction. By the third hit, I grew tired of the hassle and snapped his cane like a twig. Splinters flew everywhere.

"Chill out, old man," I yelled.

"I'll die first, boy," Pete swung his fists with all of his might.

I ducked low and scooped him from his feet. I took him into the air before slamming him down onto his back. He threw his arms around my neck as we both lied on the ground. I could feel him struggling to snap my neck. I used my upper body strength to pull us both into a sitting position before falling backwards and smashing his back against the floor.

Old Man Pete gripped his aching back and rolled over onto his stomach as I stood to my feet. I kicked him three times in his ribs. He grunted with each kick. I could see him spitting blood from his mouth as he writhed with pain.

"You ready to stop fighting, Father Time?" I asked.

"Go to hell," Pete spat a splatter of blood in my eyes before kicking me in the groin.

Before I could attempt to comfort the pain in my balls, the old man struggled to his feet and slapped me across my face with a full brief case. The heavy sack of books, supplies and files nearly broke my jaw in half. The pain shot through my head like a freight train. Everything around me blurred. I stumbled as my head grew light like a helium balloon.

"You chose the wrong town, deviant," said Pete before smacking me again with his brief case.

I stumbled so hard from the second hit that I nearly fell through an open window. Pete grabbed me by my neck and pushed my top half backwards out of the window. I hung backwards, flailing over the cold gulf coast waters.

"Rumor's too good for you, punk," said Pete. For some reason those words hit me like a ton of bricks. I loved Rumor and there was no way that I was going to let a geriatric prevent me from making her mine.

"You're wrong. Rumor's my last hope of being human. Loving that girl has given me a heart. She's just right for me." I strained and grunted while flipping Pete over me and out the window. I could hear the water splash as his old body impacted with the gulf.

I turned to see him struggling against the water's edge, trying to stay afloat. He gasped, his eyes grew wide, and his skin turned gray as he had what I could only assume was a heart attack. His dying eyes locked onto me as he slowly sunk Deeper into the water. His lifeless expression was the last that I saw of him before the waters turned black beneath the thickening of the night sky.

Every part of me ached from the exhaustion of our fight. I couldn't believe the old man had given me such a challenge. I slowly walked to Pete's restroom and stared into the mirror. I couldn't help but wonder if the old man was right about me not being good enough for Rumor. I wanted to be the type of man that she could love, but the monster in me was fighting back. I needed another dose of Rumor, so I cleaned the blood from my face to prepare for our date.

D's Journal Entry 3

I've seen the last breathe of life,
But I've never known its value,
Not until I felt the love of your heart,
That's when I knew I had to have you.
It's easy being a monster,
But it's hard to be a man,
But now that I know I have a soul,
I'm like arthritis in the devil's hand.
Who would've thought that hell's flames could ever be made
cooler?
But there's nothing more powerful than being loved by the
heart of Rumor.

CHAPTER 7

First Date

As told by Rumor

Do you remember the first time you took a look at yourself in the mirror and truly thought that you were beautiful? It's an exhilarating moment for any girl. For me it was also a defining moment. Sister Emmagene's delicate fingers massaged my scalp as her fingers made their way through each loop of my twisted hair. As my hair fell free, long wavy tresses of naturally beautiful curls framed the top half of my face perfectly. Before that moment, I hadn't realized how high my cheekbones had grown or how my skin radiantly glowed. The girl in the mirror was still me, but she was looking more like my mother every day.

"Nothing like a castor oil wash to brighten up a nappy hair day. Honey, I have out-done myself this time." Sister Emmagene smiled while stretching my shiny curls along the side of my face.

"It looks beautiful, Sister Emmagene." I smiled while taking in the sight of myself.

"You're beautiful, hun. I have to admit that when I first saw your kinky, matted head come bopping through my shop, I was a little concerned. I don't know what it is with this generation of girls rejecting the creamy crack. That brotha' Garrett Morgan put God in a bottle when he found the cure to these naps," Sister Emmagene joked.

"I was afraid too after I cut my hair, but now I realize that it was just my insecurities playing with my head. We bathe in chemicals daily trying to cover up what is unique about us. God gave us hair that locks to hold in our virtue," I explained.

"And skin that darkens to shade the purity of our souls," Sister Emmagene added.

"Exactly. I've never felt more comfortable than the day that I allowed the world to truly see me." My eyes lit up as I rubbed my fingers through the natural curls.

"Girl, you are a mess. So tell me more about this boy that you're getting all dolled up for." Sister Emmagene laughed.

"What makes you think this is about a boy?" I asked, trying to deflect her attention away from my personal life.

"This face is so beat that I know I don't look a day over 24 hours, but honey I was not born yesterday. Your nose is about as wide as all of Dixie." Sister Emmagene tilted her head to the side and twisted her lips to the left to let me know that she was not buying my innocent act.

"He's just a new friend I met at school. Don't go telling Aunt HoneyBea," I said.

"Aww that's so sweet. I just love watching you girls grow up. But speaking of your Aunt, what is going on with Beatrice? She's been acting strange lately," asked Sister Emmagene.

"She's having a hard time adjusting to everything. First Darryl Junior moved away and now Gia's gone too. I think it's just hard on her to see us all growing up so fast," I said.

"I know the feeling. It was so hard for me to send Nivea off to a boarding school after she got into all of that trouble. I miss my baby. I could be there for Beatrice, but she's been pushing me away."

"Just stick in there. If I know anything about my aunt, I know she's a very strong woman. She'll come around." I grabbed Sister Emmagene's hand to relieve the weight of the world that I could feel she was holding.

"You're wise beyond your years, hun. Hold on a minute before you leave. I have something to give you." Sister Emmagene shuffled through a drawer and pulled out an unopened condom package.

"I don't need that," I said while shooting her an awkward look.

"Just take it, hun. I know you're not planning on doing anything, but it's better to be safe than sorry." She planted a kiss on my cheek while leaving the condom in my hands. I looked down at the package and inhaled the significance of what it meant. Before that moment it wasn't really clear to me what was happening. I was preparing to travel through the uncharted territory of dating a man. That concern left me with a pack of butterflies in the pit of my stomach that followed me onto my date night with D.

From the front porch, I sat facing a large full moon. A gang of fireflies danced across Aunt HoneyBea's flower bed. Not even the fireflies with their flickering lights could compare to the constant twinkling of nerves in my stomach. I took in a lung full of fresh Mississippi air, but it wasn't even enough to clear the anxiety that plagued me. I had never been on a date before. What would I say? What was he expecting from me? Would I have to have sex? I didn't even know the first thing about sex. My worries nearly sent me into panic mode until the loud blasts of a nearby motorcycle engine nearly muted my thoughts.

I watched as a cyclist came to a stop before our driveway and removed his helmet. It was D. His dark skin nearly blended with the night, but his white eyes and teeth were like stars on Earth. He left the motorcycle resting on its kickstand as he approached the front porch. I did not move an inch. My nerves had left me frozen. It was as if I was seeing him for the first time.

"Sorry I'm late. I ran into a very old speed bump on the way." As D stepped onto the porch, he stretched his arms out toward me. The fireflies left a trail of light in between us. It was almost magical the way that they formed a path for me to embrace his hand. I was still nervous, but without speaking one word, I joined D. on the back of his bike.

With so much wind whipping in our ears, it was easy to shield my awkward nerves. As the dark blue sky and the black top meshed into the mystery of the night, I closed my eyes and gripped D.'s waist for dear life. I laid my head against his rock hard back. I could feel his tensed muscles easing beneath the comfort of my touch. Despite the fact that we were still basically strangers, I felt safer in D.'s presence than I had in a long time.

After about a half hour ride, we came to a stop at the docks. Lights from the night sky glistened against the water's surface. It was a beautiful sight. My zodiac sign is Cancer; and just like any crab, I always loved the water.

"The water seems so endless around the horizon. It makes you just want to jump in and swim into another world," I said while gazing over the edge of the docks.

"Then let's do it," said D. while pulling his shirt from the waist of his pants. As the shirt pulled over his head, finely sculpted abs seized my attention. His chiseled chest stretched as his mountainous arms threw the t-shirt onto the ground. My eyes were lost against the alluring appeal of his body. "You just gonna stand there and look or are you jumping in?"

"I'm not getting in that water. My hair's already frizzy enough from the ride to get here," I said while looking down at the ground to avoid losing my senses at the sight of his muscles.

"You don't have to worry about that. From where I'm standing, you couldn't be more gorgeous." D. slowly dampened his bottom lip with the tip of his tongue. My body filled with so much heat that I could feel my palms perspiring.

I bashfully turned away from the water to face a large and fancy-looking boat. The winds caused it to drift back and forth along the edge of the wooden docks. It was like watching a majestic cloud drift above the water's surface.

"You like that boat?" D. asked as I felt him approaching me

from behind.

"It's beautiful. Is it yours?" I asked.

"You wanted to know more about me, so I figured what's more personal to a man than his home. This is the place where I come to get away from everything. It's usually just me and the water, a situation ideal for Scorpios as well as Cancers." D.'s face lit up with a boastful smile. I could tell that he enjoyed knowing so much about me when I knew so little about him.

"You're a Scorpio? I should've known." I laughed.

"I don't know how to take that. What's wrong with being a Scorpio?" He stepped closer. I could feel his breath against the back of my neck.

"Nothing. Just making an observation." I nervously moved further away from him.

"C'mon now. You don't have to be so nervous. I'm not going to bite," he said.

"Well scorpions are known for their bite," I said.

"And so are crabs, but you don't see me complaining." Again he moved closer to me, but this time, he took my hands into his own.

"You're a man, I wouldn't expect you to." I said while finding it increasingly more difficult to avoid D.'s sex appeal.

"C'mon, there aren't many men who can bring a quiver to an angel's eyes." His tight stare grew warmer as it settled on me.

"Look, I don't know what you think this is about, but I'm not that type of chick. If you're expecting anything more than good company, you may as well take me home now." The sexual energy grew so thick within me that I snapped as a result of the frustration.

"Calm down. It looks like we got off to a bad start. How about I put my shirt back on and we step inside the boat for a bit of dinner?" he said as I nodded in agreement.

The inside of the boat was even lovelier than I imagined. The floors and paneling were all hardwood. It was fully furnished with soft plush sofas and couches, a California king-sized bed, black steel appliances, and all kinds of Egyptian décor. A path of lit candles outlined the floor. They lit a trail from the entrance to the dining room where a table was decorated with a chilled bottle of champagne and two empty plates.

"Oh my God. This is amazing. Did you do all of this for me?" I exclaimed while putting my hands over my mouth. I couldn't believe he had gone through so much trouble.

"Yes. I really care about you, Rumor. All of this is about you. You are the first person to ever make me feel like a man, a good man," he said while pulling my seat out for me.

"Nobody's ever done anything like this for me," I admitted.

"That's surprising because you deserve so much more. I hope you like shrimp and lobster tails."

"I'm a sucker for seafood, just as much as I'm a sucker for the sea." I chuckled as he dropped a bowl of butter soaked shrimp and juicy lobster tails onto my plate.

Over the glow of candlelight, I noticed cuts and bruises on D.'s face. As classically handsome as he appeared, he also had an unusually hard face for a young man. It was as if the lines of his face told a terribly tragic tale.

"What happened to your face?" I asked before biting into one of the most delicious shrimp I ever tasted.

"Nothing important. We had a little accident at the shop earlier. How is the food?"

"Delicious. You are a jack of many trades; an auto-mechanic, a cook, and a superhero all in one man."

"Well, like I said before. There's something about you that makes me better." He smirked.

"I have a feeling that you've been this way long before me. A few days ago at the school, what exactly did you say to Principal Cheadle to make him let us go?"

"When you start off as a small kid alone on the most dangerous streets, you learn how to get what you want out of people. It's called survival."

I just stared at him. It was amazing how he always knew the right things to say. Each of his words was sweet as sugar, but somehow they still left me starving for more. I had no idea who the man on the other side of the table was, and that was a fact that worried me.

"Where are you from? Why were you alone? Didn't you have a family?" I asked.

At first, he was silent. His eyes scanned the room as I saw the only sign of vulnerability that I've ever seen in them. His voice slightly cracked making it clear that he was having a hard time rehashing the events of his answer.

"I'm from New Orleans. I grew up on the streets of an area known as Da Magnolia. The only family I had was my mama, and she was just a damn crack-head. I couldn't have been older than eight, and I took more care of her than she ever did of me. If I had a dime for every time that I had to drag her whore-ass out of her own vomit or throw away her dirty needles when the cops decided to do a raid, I'd be a rich man."

"I'm sorry you went through that." I fought back tears while imagining the desperation of his childhood.

"No need to be sorry for me. I wouldn't change a thing. Growing up with that cracked out cunt made me who I am," he said.

"I know she hurt you, but she's your mother."

"Don't call her that. You had a mother. You had someone who sacrificed everything for your well-being. That's a mother. What I had was a monster. She never forfeited one moment to remind me how much she wished she had aborted me. In her eyes, I wasn't worthy of her love. The worst part about it is that she felt that way even when she was sober."

"I can't imagine that. I'm so sorry, D." I could no longer hold back my tears.

"Don't cry, angel eyes. I'm good, 'cause I got you," he said before reaching across the table to grab my hand.

The weight of his story was heavy. My desire for him to open up had dampened the mood. I felt terrible for causing him to relive such horrible moments, so I stood from the table and pulled a book from the shelf beside his bed.

"The Alchemist. I haven't seen this book since I was about four years old," I said while studying the cover of the paperback novel.

"Don't tell me that you were reading novels at the age of four. You're even smarter than I thought."

"Of course not. This was one of my mom's favorite stories. The only reason it stands out to me is because every time she'd finish reading it, she'd go on and on about how life was a treasure chest. She'd say, Rumor if you focus hard enough, you can have whatever it is that you want out of life." I smiled while stroking the book's cover.

"So what is it that Rumor wants out of life?" D. stood from the table and approached me.

"To be loved."

"To be loved? You've got your aunts and cousins."

"Not that kind of love. I want to be someone's one and only. I want to be the first thing they think about in the morning, and the last thing they pray about at night." I said while looking up into his eyes. My reflection in his eyes was like the answer to my desires. From his perspective, I was an angel. I was the only love he had ever known, and in that moment, that was all that mattered.

"I love you, Rumor." D. pulled me into his embrace. My lips thirsted for his. My hands read the words of his body language like braille. I was no longer afraid. I kissed him passionately while leaving my body open to unveiling.

D. opened me physically and spiritually as if I were a delicate, but valuable package. With intensity, his love ravaged my body. I was overcome with ecstasy simply from the anticipation of his touch. He pulled my blouse over my head, and kissed me from my lips to my chest. With his lips against my breast, D. laid eyes on the black cat diamond that hung from a necklace down into my bra.

D. paused to gawk at the flawless surface of the diamond, "What's this?"

"A symbol," I answered.

"A symbol of what?"

"My strength," I said as he threw me onto the soft mattress of the king-sized bed. While standing over me, he removed his shirt to reveal his muscular chest. I pulled the condom package from my pocket, and he seized it from my hand.

"Are you sure you want to do this?" he asked.

"Yes," my voice purred with the seduction of the moment as D. delved deeply into my soul. The pleasure was unexplainable. It was like an out-of-body experience. It was as if our souls levitated towards the Gulf of Mexico and danced across the Pacific Ocean.

Rumor's Journal Entry 4

Pledge the plight of the caterpillar.
Is his love the wings to her butterfly?
Or will he salt her beneath the sun,
To make her ooze before she dries?
Will she soar by the means of splendor,
After she has allowed him to shatter her cocoon?
Or will she crawl amongst the hurt,
Of opening her heart way too soon?

CHAPTER 8

Tulips and Weeds

As Told By Rumor

Aunt Honeybea always said that your day can be full of tulips or garden weeds, because if you push aside enough flowers you'll always find a few weeds. Tulips were the good times. They were the moments that made us smile. The weeds were everything else that made life difficult every once in a while. While lying in bed next to the first man that I ever romantically loved, I blushed at the sight of life's newest tulip.

The morning sun peaked through the blades of the window shade and glistened across his dark chocolate skin. While Deep in slumber, he turned and left his head resting against my chest. I brushed my hand against the tiny hairs of his five o' clock shadow. My bare skin was bathed by the sensation of his warm breath as he softly snored. A tiny vein bulged from his forehead with the rhythm of his heart-beat. While in my arms, he was at peace. I couldn't take my eyes off of him. He was mine, and I belonged to him.

As I caressed his face, I found beauty in every inch of it. Even the scars, bruises, and harsh signs of a tough life were alluring to me. It was the perfect moment until my fingers glided across D.'s nightmare. I felt the beating vein on his forehead begin to bulge at a more rapid rate. His head jerked a couple times as his closed eyelids clinched together. His pupils rolled around beneath his lids like demolition trucks. His entire body trembled causing the bed to shake beneath us both. I moved my hand from his face to his arms. I gently felt the marked skin of his tattoos. I used them as a guide to console his nightmares. At first, it worked. His heartbeat grew steadier.

Just as I released a sigh of relief, he blurted out words that sent chills down my spine, "Just die, mama!" His tone was filled with pure hatred. His words felt like acid as they burned through my tranquility. His voice added an extra amount of authority to the word "die" that left me wondering. He made it clear that he had been abused by his mother, but I never thought to ask him what happened to her.

"D., wake up." I shook him repeatedly, trying to release him from his nightmares.

No matter how hard I shook him, his eyes remained closed. But his mind was hardly resting.

All of a sudden, he leapt on top of me and pushed the weight of his forearm into my throat. I tried to get him off of me, but he was too strong. I gagged and struggled for air, but I couldn't muster one scream as his arm cut off my air supply. I could feel the tears streaming from the sides of my eyes down to my ears. My senses melted as all of the life drained from me. The excruciating pain led to a frightening numbness as the bones of my neck snapped in several places. My skin felt as if I were in freezing weather. My vision darkened, but somehow the lines of rage on D.'s face never left my sight. I couldn't believe that love had become my introduction to death.

Moments later, I screamed while jolting forward from the bed. The sheets were all soaked with my sweat. I quivered uncontrollably as I looked up to see D. facing me. I was relieved to see that he was wide awake and my neck was still intact.

"You okay, angel eyes? You over there sweating harder than a hoe in church." The look of concern on his face and the sound of my own breathing made it clear that it had all been a nightmare.

"I'm fine, babe," I said as I returned his embrace. There was no way I was about to look past my tulips for a bunch of nightmare weeds.

Ignoring those weeds proved to be very beneficial, because that morning started with more than enough tulips. It was about five in the morning when D. took me home. Aunt HoneyBea didn't notice a thing. In fact, she never came out of her room once as I skipped through the house while getting ready for school. I danced to the music of my alarm clock's radio while picking out the cutest outfit. I even flat ironed my own hair, which is something that I usually hate doing. I sat in front of my vanity mirror and shook my heat-treated hair from left to right. With my comb in hand, I parted and braided my hair into two fishtail braids. I winked at myself as I posed in the mirror because I loved the woman before me.

That's when Right Said Fred's "I'm Too Sexy" song blasted through the radio's speakers. I stood on top of the chair as the mirror reflected my full image. D. had made me a woman, and the after-glow of his love looked amazing on me. My breasts were extra perky, and my waist was the size of a pea. For the first time ever my hips were growing out; and if I arched my back just right, I noticed a slight curve in my butt. I've always been cute, but on that particular day, I was sexy. I held my comb to my mouth and lip-synced while twirling before the mirror.

The day just kept getting better. At school, I arrived to a welcoming committee. Half the girls had cut their hair to go natural. It felt like I was walking onto a campus full of fierce freedom. Every single one of them spoke to me and asked me about my braids. They went on and on about how they enjoyed my spirit performance at the pep rally. Many of them even showed me pictures of Rima's face as I accepted the spirit stick. They all loved me. I couldn't believe it, but I had dethroned Rima. In only a few days, I had become the most popular girl in school.

"Hey Rumor. Girl, where have you been?" Candace came pushing her way through my pack of afro dolls.

"Girl, I love your hair. You gotta show me how to do that braid." Natalie stepped to Candace's side.

"Really? But you both hate me, right?" I looked at them both with unwavering suspicion in my eyes.

"Hate? Girl, we love you." Candace said.

"Ok crazy ladies, it's time to break up this little casting call for Single Black Female. Don't call us and we damn sure won't be calling you." Tami barked at the crowd of girls.

"Hey Tami," said Natalie.

"Don't speak to me, tramp. Go find some other ass to kiss. Rumor's is closed for renovations," snarked Tami.

"But Tami!" Candace exclaimed.

"Step, minions," shouted Tami as Candace and Natalie scurried away.

"Rumor, you have turned this school all the way out." Kayla smiled at the sight of so many natural girls.

"Me? You brought the natural trend to Mississippi. I was just following your lead," I said.

"No, honey, I just showed you that it was possible. You plowed that lane all on your own." Kayla's face clearly displayed her pride in my growth.

"Whatever. Enough with all the mushy stuff. I got some tea so good you gonna need to sit down to sip on this." Tami pointed towards a picnic table just outside out of the cafeteria. It was behind an unkempt, bushy tree, and just stealthy enough for Tami to feel comfortable with her daily gossip.

"So what's going on Tami?" I asked as we all settled into our seats.

"Ok, so girl, have you heard about the smash list?" Tami was so expressive when it came to her gossip. She opened and closed her hands as if they were speaking for her.

"The what kind of list?" Kayla interjected.

"You're from New York, so you have an excuse. But Rumor, where the hell have you been? It's like the biggest thing on Facebook right now," Tami explained.

"Tami, you know I'm not big on Facebook," I admitted.

"Well now you're a hot topic, so you need to catch up with the rest of the world. Every month, the biggest ballas in Mississippi update a list of the top 10 most smashable chicks of the delta. Guess who just made number one." Tami's eyes stuck to me like a dart to a board.

"Hold on, let me get this right. These backwards bastards of Mississippi are rating vaginas and Rumor is at the top of the list?" Kayla asked.

"Ding! Ding! Ding, Veronica Mars! Did you figure that one out all on your own?" Tami said sarcastically.

"Yeah, but what I can't figure out is how is this good news," said Kayla.

"Aye, don't knock it 'til you tried it. You're looking at January's Most Smashable, baby. It's not easy being the baddest chick, but somebody's gotta do it." Tami smiled.

"Tami, you crazy." I laughed.

"Look, you can't be a virgin the rest of your life. Your 16th birthday is this weekend. You're gonna have to eventually open that pocketbook for somebody. This month, you have your pick of the litter," said Tami. The crazy thing is that with everything going on, I'd forgotten all about my birthday.

"She doesn't have to open anything." Kayla's frustration was beginning to show on her face.

"Excuse me, but is your name Rumor? Who died and made you her vagina's keeper?" said Tami.

"Kayla, don't let Tami get you all worked up. She's just joking," I said.

"The hell I am. Medusa is starting to get on my nerves," said Tami.

"Medusa? You know what your problem is, Tami?" said Kayla.

"What's my problem, boo?" Tami stood to her feet and leaned forward to greet Kayla face-to-face.

"You're so used to everyone giving you a pass on class because your last name is Tahiri. Well let me tell you something, honey. There's only so far you're going to go in life by just showing your black ass!" Kayla shouted.

"Girl, don't worry about my black ass. You need to check your attitude because right now it smells like something that just fell out of your flat ass!" Tami shot back with a vengeance.

"Will you two please chill out?" I plead.

"You know what? I think I'll hold off on drop kicking Medusa for now. What do you think, Rumor? Do you want to spend the rest of your life being a virgin or are you ready to bring your 16th in with some fun?" Tami blocked Kayla's face with her open hand before turning to question me.

"Oh my God, Tami. I don't want to talk about this," I said.

"Wait just a damn minute. What was that?" Tami exclaimed.

"What was what?" I asked as Tami looked closely into my eyes.

"You're not telling me something, Rumor Arden. In fact, we've been sitting here all this time and you ain't mentioned your date with D. once." Tami observed.

"It was ok. There's nothing much to talk about. Besides, when was I supposed to say anything? The two of you have been going back and forth like cats and dogs."

"Nah, boo. You're glowing, and you've had that same stupid smile on your face all morning. D. popped your cherry, didn't he?"

Tami excitedly stated. The bushes behind us ruffled as if they too were excited.

"Tami, why are you so loud. Calm down," I said.

"Rumor, is this true?" Kayla asked.

"Hell yea, it's true. I know my girl." Tami smiled.

I turned around and inspected the bush tree behind us. I was sure that I heard something moving. The last thing I needed was the whole school knowing about my new-found love life.

"Girl, ain't nobody back there? It was probably just a little bird or something," said Tami while pulling me away from the bushes and back to her interrogation.

"How much do you know about this boy? You just met him the other day," said Kayla.

"She knows enough. Dang, are you her mother or something?" Tami's irritation with Kayla got the best of her. We rarely spoke about my mother. Everyone knew that she was a pretty sore subject for me, so Tami immediately clasped her hands against her mouth. "I'm sorry, Rumor."

"It's fine. The bell will be ringing soon. I'm just going to get a head start to class," I said while walking away from them both. As hard as it was to hear, Tami's words were actually on point. Kayla's concerns were starting to remind me of my mother. I wasn't sure if she'd be proud of my decision to sleep with D. or not. The words of her song had taught me to protect my heart or watch it burn, but instead I chose to give my heart to a strange man. What scared me most was that I had no idea whether he would protect my heart or light the match that would finally set it ablaze.

Meanwhile the weeds in my life were persistently attempting to grow, but as I stopped to open my locker, I discovered a beautiful arrangement of actual tulips. The flowers appeared to be flavors of ice cream: purples, pinks, yellows and whites mixed with Baby's Breath. It was gorgeous. There was a small note attached, but it only read, "Happy Birthday." I had no idea who they were from, but I automatically assumed them to be a message from D. I hadn't told him about my birthday, but D was crafty and already knew so much about me. I closed my locker door and leaned against it with stars in my eyes. I inhaled the scent of the flowers and found myself overcome with nothing but pleasant thoughts.

"Rumor Arden, report to the principal's office immediately." A voice blasted through the school's PA system. The first bell hadn't even rang. It was too early in the morning for me to have already found trouble.

As I entered Principal Cheadle's office, I was surprised to see Aunt HoneyBea sitting in front of his desk. I had no idea why she was there. Aunt HoneyBea hadn't been called to the school since sixth grade when I fought all three of the Tahiri triplets. With my flowers in hand, I stood facing the disappointed looks of Aunt HoneyBea and Principal Cheadle.

"Rumor, do you have any idea why we called you to my office?" Principal Cheadle asked before I could even sit down.

"Honestly I don't," I answered.

"Lil girl, don't play stupid. I can't believe you got these people calling me up here to this school. You know you ain't too big for me to put some heat to that behind of yours," Aunt HoneyBea fussed.

"What did I do?" I asked.

"You just come with us, young lady." Principal Cheadle stood from his chair and ushered us out of his office. As we walked through the hallway, I could feel Aunt HoneyBea's stare burning a hole in my back. I scrambled through my head trying to figure out why I was in so much trouble. It had to be the mushrooms. Principal Cheadle must've told Aunt HoneyBea everything, and she was going to kill me for sure.

We came to a stop before the teacher's lounge. Aunt HoneyBea turned to me with her hand on her hip. That stance assured me that she meant business. "You have anything to say for yourself before we open this door, lil girl."

I only shook my head as a reply.

"SURPRISE!" As they opened the door, the lounge was filled with students, teachers, family, friends and church members who had all gathered to celebrate my birthday. I couldn't believe it. It was a surprise party.

Everyone cleared a path to reveal a large three-tier cake with butterflies cascading down the left hand side. Their wings were lit with candles, each of which represented one of my sixteen years of life. Behind the cake, there were several gift bags and colorfully wrapped boxes. Many balloons floated all across the room. It was an overwhelming sight to see so much joy and celebration in my name.

My eyes filled with tears as I walked the path toward the cake. Almost everyone had a spray can of silly string, and they all doused me with the contents of their canisters. I could see their mouths moving as they all sung the birthday song, but I could not hear one sound over the happiness beaming from within me. Tami playfully threw her head from side-to-side while smiling and jumping with excitement. Kayla leaned forward with a huge smile and her mouth swelled from what could have only been a glorious shout. Sister Emmagene waved and blew kisses as if I were royalty. I was even surprised to see that my Uncle Champ had gotten all clean and dapper to join in on the festivities. He gave me a quick hug before shooting a trail of silly string across my forehead. Right before I reached the cake, I looked to see Taylor somberly smiling and nodding in my direction.

"Okay baby girl, wish hard and blow even harder. Auntie needs you to put out those candles before they call the fire department." Aunt HoneyBea whispered in my ear from behind as we both faced the cake.

I cleared the silly string and tears from my face before closing my eyes. In that moment, there was only one thing that I could wish for. To some it may have been a foolish wish, but all I wanted for my birthday was the chance to see my mother both living and breathing once again. Behind closed eyes, I could see her beautiful smile. Her eyes twinkled as she mouthed the words, "Happy Birthday." Without hesitation, I blew all of my joy, love, and wishes onto those candles. My breath blew across that cake like a cool summer breeze until every flame became a small puff of smoke.

Aunt HoneyBea stood in the center of the teacher's lounge and commanded everyone's attention. "I want to thank each and every one of you for coming out today to help me celebrate God's gift of Rumor Arden. I cannot express how much of a blessing this child has been to me. From the moment she was born, she brought so much love to my home. It was a love that brought some much needed healing to a very broken family. I never was able to have children of my own, but God still saw fit to bless me with Rumor and her cousins. There is not a day that goes by in which I don't drop to my knees and thank the Lord for my precious Rumor."

"Thank you auntie." I raced into her arms for a hug so tight and warm; the type that only Aunt HoneyBea could provide.

"Where is the music? It's time to turn up." With Tami's words, the party commenced. Everyone raced to the center of the lounge. We danced the electric slide, the cha cha slide, and whatever other steps that we knew at the time. Everyone seemed to be enjoying themselves, except for Taylor who I noticed was secluded to a corner alone.

I excused myself from the dance floor and joined Taylor on the other side of the lounge. "Ay redbone, come on out to this dance floor and let big mama put a smile on your face," I said trying to pull a smile from his heavy heart, but Taylor was clearly not in the mood.

"Enjoy your party. I'm feeling a lil' tired. I'm about to head back to class." Taylor mumbled.

"You can't leave, it's my birthday," I said.

"Your birthday is Saturday. I'll give you a call." Taylor attempted to walk past me.

"Taylor, what's going on? Talk to me." I grabbed his arm and gave him my best pair of puppy dog eyes.

"You had sex with him, Rumor?" I was frozen stiff with chills as the words left his mouth.

"How do you know that?" I whispered. Taylor glanced over my shoulder and I followed his eyes in Rima's direction. She waved with a big, stupid smile on her face. That's when it occurred to me that the little bird from the bushes was sporting a nine-inch weave.

"So it's true? I warned you about that dude and your reaction was to go sleep with him?"

"Taylor, it wasn't like that," I said.

"Then, tell me what it was like, because I'm having a hard time with this whole thing. I'm standing here with a big knot on the back of my head where someone knocked me out in the locker room last night. The funny thing is that I was supposed to meet up with Old Man Pete about your boyfriend, and now conveniently I can't even get the old man to answer the phone."

"You had D. investigated? C'mon Taylor. That's a bit much," I protested.

"Did you get anything else out of what I just said? Your boyfriend is a psychopath, but you refuse to see that. I'm done trying to protect you," Taylor retorted.

"Protect me? No one asked for your protection. You're just jealous because finally I have someone who loves me," I snapped.

"Look, I don't want to ruin your party. I'm just gonna leave," Taylor said before pulling away from me and walking out of the lounge.

My friendship with Taylor had taken many hits over the last few days, but that moment was different. There was more pain in his eyes than I had ever seen from him before. The crazy thing was that my first true love came with the price of Taylor's pain. I realized that D. and Taylor were like salt and water. I couldn't have them both. Embracing one meant forsaking the other. By allowing Taylor to walk out of that lounge, I feared that he would never forgive me.

"Is everything okay? I hope Taylor's tantrum didn't ruin your party." Rima smiled with a disgusting amount of satisfaction.

Walking away was the only thing I could do to keep from hitting her. I needed some fresh air, so I stepped outside the school. Most everyone was either in class or at my party, so it was very quiet outside until I overheard Aunt HoneyBea's phone conversation.

"I just spoke to the doctor the other day. I don't have a lot of time. I need to be sure that everything is in place for Rumor to receive her inheritance," said Aunt HoneyBea. What did she mean about not having a lot of time? And what inheritance was I receiving?

"No, she doesn't know. No one does. I want to keep it that way. I'll tell them all when I'm ready. She's been through a lot already without having to find out that her aunt has breast cancer." I nearly fell from my feet. I had to be dreaming. There was no way she said what I thought I heard. Aunt HoneyBea was supposed to always be there. She was all I had left. There was no way I'd be able to go on without her.

When I returned to my party, my hands were shaking with fear. People were talking to me, but I couldn't concentrate on a word they were saying. There was a dark feeling in the pit of my stomach that I just couldn't overcome. My legs were so weak that I had to take a seat. I tried to muster enough smiles to keep people's concerns at bay, but my cheeks were numb. I could not feel anything but despair.

I leaned forward to contain the painful nerves that were building within my stomach. It felt as if a nest of hornets were stinging me all at once. I took several large breaths, but none of them could cleanse my body of the shock.

"It's interesting to see a victim wearing the symbol of her threat. This must be some form of Stockholm syndrome." The voice was so deep and disturbing that in my delirium, I initially confused him for the devil. Although later, I would find that my conclusion wasn't very far from the truth. The man was peering down my blouse at the black cat diamond which secretly hung across my chest. His voice and expressions were beyond creepy. I threw my hands over my blouse to conceal my chest from his prying eyes.

His eyes were like windows to bitter hatred. Between the lines of contempt that marked his face were horrid shadows. I was already too full of anguish to receive the negative vibes that his presence was sending me. All I could do was stare as the venom of his words dripped onto the floor before me, "I guess the black cat's got your tongue. Well, there will be plenty of time for us to become acquainted later. It hasn't been announced yet, but you're looking at the new head minister at the Rock of the Delta First Missionary Baptist Church."

As if my hearing hadn't been stained with enough bad news, he dropped a major bomb on me. Not only did I have to deal with the end of my friendship with Taylor and Aunt HoneyBea's cancer, but on top of everything else, my father's legacy had just been handed to a creepy stranger.

"I'll catch you later, kitten." He exploded into a laugh that was similar to the struggling gasps of a dying man. It was just a reminder that no tulip could ever drown out the devastation left by the overwhelming amount of weeds in my life.

Rumor's Journal Entry 5

It's hard to enjoy the flight,
When you're busy waiting for the fall.
Because even when you're happy,
You're still afraid to lose it all.
Even the smallest problems,
Will seem extra tall,
When you're looking through the fun house glass,
Of a wicked crystal ball.
I've lost a lot of good fortune,
On bets I was too afraid to call,
So I cannot continue to live my life
With my back against the wall.

CHAPTER 9

Finding Gia
As Told By Rumor

If Aunt HoneyBea was rice, then I had become the color white because I was determined not to leave her alone. I searched through every inch of our house for some sign of her condition, but my aunt had obviously covered her tracks. There was absolutely nothing in her mail but some grocery store coupons and her normal bills. I couldn't find one prescription in her medicine cabinet. If I hadn't heard her phone conversation for myself, I would've sworn she was perfectly healthy.

"Rumor, I need you to watch your Aunt Mildred. I'm about to run a few errands." Aunt HoneyBea hurried towards the front door with her large purse in hand.

"Wait a minute, auntie. I wanna come." I said while racing to her side.

"Girl, I'll be right back. Just watch Mildred for me." Aunt HoneyBea said before quickly shutting the door behind her.

I was not about to let her out of my sight. I hurried to Aunt HoneyBea's room to see Aunt Mildred rocking away in her chair. She seemed to be asleep, so I found my old bicycle and took off in pursuit of Aunt HoneyBea. It wasn't hard keeping up with Aunt HoneyBea who always drove like an old woman. It was however hard to avoid her spotting me as I pedaled through traffic with the speed of a champion horseback rider. She drove across several neighborhoods to a red brick house that I recognized as Deacon Booker's home.

That's when I realized that Deacon Booker was not at my party, so I figured that he must've been the one she was talking to on the phone. I snuck around the house to the backdoor which was unsurprisingly open. People in Hurley were so comfortable in their neighborhoods that you could find most of us sleeping with our windows and doors open. I tiptoed my way in through the kitchen. I could hear their voices as they spoke, but I didn't understand one word of their exchange. As I tried to get slightly closer, I heard footsteps approaching from upstairs.

"I'm late. Where are my keys? Honey, have you seen my keys?" Sheila Owen yelled while scrambling through the house in search for her keys.

"Check your coat pockets," said Deacon Booker.

"Wow, that man knows me better than I know myself." Said Ms. Owen while she pulled the keys from her pocket. I quickly ducked into a broom closet as she hurried out the front door.

"Well, I guess I'll be on my way as well. Thanks for helping me handle this paperwork, Brother Booker," said Aunt HoneyBea.

"Anytime, Sister HoneyBea. I'm praying for you and your family. I hope you know that you're not in this alone," said Deacon Booker.

"I know, Deacon. You and Sister Owen have been a godsend." Aunt HoneyBea stood in the doorway of Deacon Booker's home office and smiled. I hid back inside of the closet just in time for her to depart through the front door.

Once I heard the ignition of her Cadillac roar, I knew that Aunt HoneyBea had left the front yard. I stood from hiding and made my way toward Deacon Booker's office. I was fed up with all the secrets, and it couldn't have been clearer that the Deacon had answers.

I could tell that Ms. Owen was responsible for Deacon Booker's furniture and decorations; his place wasn't exactly your typical bachelor's pad. Tiny glass cherubim, crucifixes, and unicorns were placed on end tables, counters, the edges of the fire place, and on top of wooden wall mounts; the walls were all covered with copies of classic abstract paintings; cream colored plush carpeting was laid across hard wood flooring; a cream leather sectional sofa framed the entire living room perfectly; and leafy flowers sprouted from pots placed behind each corner of the sectional. As calming as it all appeared, I couldn't help but feel overwhelming anger as I approached the Deacon's office.

Deacon Booker's office was nothing like the rest of his home; it was horribly junky. There were no pictures on the wall at all. One framed degree was nailed directly above his head, but everything else was disheveled paperwork. Beneath all of those files, folders, and supplies thrown any and everywhere, there was a hardly visible desk, and Deacon Booker sat behind it intensely focused on his thoughts.

"Ahem." I loudly cleared my throat to gain his attention.

"Rumor, how'd you get here?" Deacon Booker, surprised to see me, stood from his desk.

"Don't stand. Have a seat. I have a feeling this may take a while," I said.

"What are you talking about? How did you get in?" he asked.

"Does my aunt have cancer?" As if I hadn't heard his question, I proceeded with my own.

"It's not my place to say. That's something you should speak with HoneyBea about?"

"She's all I have left. This town has already stolen everything else from me. Why won't you tell me?" My voice started to crack as the emotional build-up ripped away at me from the inside.

"I'm sorry," He said with sorrow in his eyes.

"No, you're not. You came to me for help in restoring my father's legacy. Do you remember that?" Tears slowly ran down my face.

"I do and I will forever be grateful to you for that. This entire town is grateful."

"Then why are you selling out my father's legacy to some criminal in a suit?" I screamed. I could tell by the shock in his eyes that he knew exactly who I was referring to.

"Rumor, please have a seat." Deacon Booker stood to his feet and leaned against his messy desk as papers slid onto the floor. "I owe you an explanation. I hoped it wouldn't come out this way. I wanted to speak to you first."

"Who is he?" I asked.

"His name is Nefarius Grimm. I don't know much about him, outside of the fact that I owe him a huge debt," Deacon Booker explained.

"Why?" I said.

He took a Deep breath before answering me. I could tell that something was eating away at him. His eyes were filled with moisture and his hands were shaking uncontrollably. I was almost afraid to hear what he had to say, but I courageously waited for his answer anyway.

"It's been tough managing the church without your father. The black cat diamonds helped a lot, but after Hurricane Veronya, the people of Hurley haven't been able to tithe. We were going to lose the church. I didn't know what else to do," the Deacon cried.

"What did you do?" I spoke with anticipation.

"Sheila and I searched through the financial books looking for solutions. We came across some strange entries that Lula Mae had made. It looked as if she was able to borrow some funds from a church in New Orleans, so we took a trip to the bayou."

"And the church gave you the money?" I asked intensely.

"They had no idea who we were. They had never heard of the church or of Lula Mae Johnson. We couldn't believe it. That was our last option. We were ready to just pack our bags and give up until a large creepy man whistled for our attention. It was Nefarius. He offered to give us the money that we needed in exchange for our services. All we had to do was deliver a duffle bag of money to an apartment in Magnolia projects."

"I'm familiar with the place. I hear it's a very rough neighborhood." I said while recalling that D. was from the Magnolia.

"Exactly. We figured it would be an easy way to make money for the church. We're church people, so there was no way anyone would suspect us of any criminal activity. It was supposed to be an easy drop-off, but everything went wrong," he explained with fear in his voice. "It was late. Sheila and I were both afraid. Nefarius had given us a gun for our protection. At first I refused to carry it, but he persuaded me by convincing me that I needed it to protect Sheila. That's where it all went wrong." The Deacon sobbed like a baby.

"It's okay, Deacon." I tried to comfort him.

"It's not okay. It'll never be okay again. Some kid jutted out of nowhere. I didn't see him coming. Sheila screamed, I panicked, and I shot him. He was only a child, and I killed him."

I was speechless. I couldn't believe the things that he was telling me. Deacon Booker was not a murderer. He was one of the kindest men I'd ever met. It felt like some sort of sick joke. It was all too surreal.

"All I could think about was the church. We were there on official church business. There was no way the church would survive the scandal, so Nefarius assured us that he would handle everything. A few days later, we were watching the news and a white New Orleans police officer was being accused of shooting a black child. The boy's name was Nicholas Macon, and Sheila and I both recognized him to be the same little boy that I had shot."

"This can't be true. You're lying," I said.

"I wish I were. I intended on taking that secret to the grave. I was never supposed to tell anyone, but it's been killing me. It's been killing me slowly and now I'm afraid I've given my best friend's church to the devil himself. I messed up and there's nothing I can do to fix it."

"What do you mean there's nothing you can do? An innocent man is on trial for this. You have to tell the police what really happened," I said.

"I want to, Rumor. I really do, but if I confess, I'm afraid to think of what Nefarius will do to Sheila. I'm trapped. It's too late for me. My soul is going to hell and Nefarius Grimm is my devil."

"There has to be something we can do," I cried.

"No, I didn't tell you all of this to involve you. Stay away from that man. Your aunt needs you right now. If you want to do something, then reunite your family so that you can all support your aunt. She needs her family now more than ever," Deacon Booker explained.

As much as I hated to admit it, Deacon Booker was right. There was nothing I could do to help him, but Aunt HoneyBea needed our family right now. I was the only one left who could bring us all together. With Darryl Junior being hundreds of miles away, I decided to start with Gia.

Gia's feminist group was strictly secluded. They were like a bunch of amazons on their own island. I knew that I needed help getting to her, and one person in particular came to mind.

"Babe, you usually don't hear about people wanting to break into a prison." D. looked at me as if I was out of my mind.

"It's not a prison. It's a feminist camp." I said rolling my eyes.

"Same difference. It's a community of same-sex societal rejects. That sounds like just about any American prison to me," he said.

"Never mind. If you're going to be a smart aleck about it, I'll just do it on my own."

"We both know you can't pull this off on your own. Besides, I could use the practice to keep my skills sharp."

"Really? What skills?" I asked.

"The key to a good hustle is all about misdirection. If I keep telling you that my orange is blue, eventually you'll start to doubt the color of the fruit that is right in front of your eyes." D. threw a fresh orange into my hands.

My hands and eyes studied the surface of the orange as I held it with both hands. Most people would've thought D.'s claims for manipulation to be a load of rubbish, but I knew better. My entire life had been defined by misdirection. I always found myself at the short end of someone's lie. Deception had become the foundation of my life, so in that moment, it was time for me to maintain that foundation with a few lies of my own.

"So how do you suggest that we misdirect this pack of SHE MEN?" I smiled a signal of agreement to whatever plans D.'s mind was concocting.

After piling on a few pounds of hot, sweaty body padding, tons of make-up, wide-framed glasses, and a long haired wig, I barely recognized the sight of myself. D called in a couple of favors to get me a fake I.D. I was pretending to be a Euro-African by the name of Yuri Abdul. Apparently I had barely escaped a Russian hostel controlled by Nazi men with my life. And ever since that day, I despised the sight of any man.

"Let me hear the Abdul story one more time," said D.

"I don't think this is a good idea," I whimpered from beneath the itchy padding.

"You'll do great. Stop being so nervous."

"Have you heard my Russian accent? I sound like Yoda."

"You're the one who wanted to talk to your cousin. This is what's going to get you on the inside. I don't care if your Russian accent sounds like speaking in tongues, you better get in there and sell it." D.'s motivational speech was about as good as a Marine drill sergeants, but somehow it worked.

The enclosed feminist camp stood out like a mole on the rest of the college campus. I felt as if I were approaching a foreign embassy by the way the girls all stood around eyeing me. Their faces were frozen into intimidating scowls. There was an air of superiority among them. A girl with arms almost as big as D.'s was the first to approach me. From the way she strutted towards me, I was initially inclined to think that she was a man. She had cornrows, wore saggy jeans, and chewed on a toothpick better than my Uncle Champ ever did.

"You must've made a wrong turn somewhere, lil' mama. SHE MAN is no place for shrimp." She stood flexing her large arms and cracking her massive knuckles. The other girls immediately stood by her side. It wasn't long before they all circled around me like a venue of vultures hungry for a fresh corpse.

"I just wanna speak to the woman in charge," I stammered over my butchered Russian accent.

"You hear that, ladies? She wants to talk to the woman in charge. We are all women in charge, so speak," she barked at me.

"Somber down, Kanetra." A thick Swedish accent spoke from behind the girls. As they all turned to face the source of the voice, a leather and chains wearing vixen stepped to the forefront.

"But Head Mistress the girls and I were just having a little fun," said Kanetra folding her massive arms across her flat chest.

"Report to PT. The little chubby one and I have some things to discuss," ordered the Head Mistress as all the girls left the two of us alone.

Her name was Head Mistress Harlot. She stood at a height of over six feet tall with breasts as big as watermelons and hips shaped like the Rock of Gibraltar. Her head was shaved into a boyish buzz cut, but thick mascara, dangling earrings, and blood red lipstick gave a feminine appeal to her face. She appeared to be in her late fifties, but she was very fit and youthful for her age. The constant squeaking of her leather attire and the sharp tapping of her sky high heels distracted me as she led me down a very long hallway. At the end of the hallway was a dark, unmarked door. I was quiet as a church mouse while watching her pull a set of keys from her waist-belt. She opened the door and behind it was a small room with glass walls that revealed, what appeared to be, a military-grade training camp for women.

My mouth dropped. It was like something out of a movie. Girls raced across rows of truck tires, curled heavy dumbbells, climbed several feet of rough rope, and blasted rounds of gun-fire on a mini-shooting range. I instantly scanned the scene for signs of Gia, but she was nowhere to be seen.

"What is this?" I asked while trying to maintain my fake accent.

"This culture of masculine monstrosities has left a scarlet letter on the faces of so many women. The funny thing is that I came to this country with high hopes. Back in Sweden, everyone bragged about this land of freedom where equal opportunity was available to everyone. I couldn't wait to witness such a magical place, but unfortunately they forgot to mention that such sentiments are reserved for those with a penis," said Head Mistress Harlot.

"This is not what I expected to see in a feminist camp."

"A feminist camp? That is laughable. Femininity is a word to describe the weak. SHE MAN is more masculine than any man. We are strong and superior, and through warfare, we plan to place our stamp across this world," she explained.

"Warfare?" I gasped.

"Yes and international terrorism. Something a Russian expatriate would clearly understand, which by the sound of your subpar accent you clearly are not." With one swing of her arm, Mistress Harlot yanked the wig and glasses from my face. "Welcome Rumor Arden. Today you will find that your journey has taken you full circle."

"Look, I just want to speak to my cousin Gia, that's all. I promise I won't tell anyone about anything that I've seen here." I shrunk with fear beneath the Head Mistress' enormous stature.

"I've waited so long to meet you, Rumor. Your grandmother told me that you have what I want, something I have spent decades searching for. You see, Viola Grimm, a woman that you know as Vendetta Gatto, was once my partner in crime. We were elite thieves who plagued the crime bosses of New York City, but Viola betrayed me for a man. After we stole a beautiful necklace of black cat shaped diamonds from the wife of mafia boss Marvin Gambino, he kidnapped Viola and ransomed her for the return of the diamonds. I was no fool. I knew that the only way I would be able to save my partner was to kill Gambino, and I did," she explained.

"I didn't even know the woman as my grandmother. She tried to have me killed, so believe me when I say we weren't close at all," I said while covering my shirt's collar with my right hand. Mistress Harlot's story made it clear that she was looking for the black diamonds, and the last thing I wanted was for her to spot it dangling around my neck.

"I know this. I paid her a visit during her final days in the hospital. She confessed it to me as I strangled the life from her dying body. It was so satisfying to watch the old witch choke. I was so much younger than her during our days as thieves, but I admired her strength, ambition, and beauty. I was the muscle and she was undoubtedly the brains, but the thing about brains is that they always eventually move on to new muscle. Viola partnered with Charlie Morello, the head of the Colombo family and a long time enemy of Marvin Gambino. The two of them fell in love and had a child. Viola became Vendetta Gatto and rose to the status of mafia queen, but she left me behind and took the jewels with her."

"I'm really sorry to hear that, but what does any of this have to do with me?" I asked.

"I'll make it simple. Give me the diamonds or I kill you," the Head Mistress threatened.

"I don't have them," I said.

"Fine. Your choice." She snapped before pulling out a sharp blade and thrusting it against my throat. I screamed for my life, but those screams were quickly interrupted by the sound of the shut door falling from its hinges.

D. leapt through the door like a lion. Head Mistress Harlot's eyes nearly popped from their sockets as she saw him. He shoved her against the glass wall as I fell to the floor beneath them.

"Rumor, get out of here. Follow the hallway to the last room on your right. Gia's in there." He struggled to speak while wrestling the knife from the Head Mistress's hands.

"So this is your latest hustle, D? How cute." Head Mistress Harlot screamed while shoving him away and punching him with her hard gloved knuckles.

D. struck her back as their struggle grew into an all-out fight. I wanted to help D., but I was sure he could handle his own. I had to find Gia. By the sounds of Harlot's terrorist intentions, Gia had bitten off way more than she could chew with her new feminist group.

I followed D.'s direction, but while racing down the hallway, I managed to run into my Gia. She wore a black shirt and gray fatigue pants. Her hair was cut into a short pixie cut, and her face was expressionless. It seemed as if she was looking straight through me.

"Gia, we gotta get out of here," I said while reaching for her arm.

"Go home, Rumor. This place ain't safe for you," said Gia with an almost monotone voice.

"You're coming with me, right? These people are crazy. I know that you're going through some things, but this is not you."

"It's me now. I'm nothing but a scandalous topic to Hurley. I'm the fast lil' heifer who came between the sheriff's boys, but Ron's a damn hero in New Orleans. It's funny how a man and woman can make the same mistake, but the woman is the only one who pays for it," Gia explained.

"I understand what you're saying. The same thing happened to my mama, but that's the purpose of family. We have to help each other through this stuff. Aunt HoneyBea needs us right now."

"SHE MAN is my family now, so just go home!" Gia fiercely stated.

"I'm not leaving without you. Did you hear anything that I just said? Our aunt needs us. She has breast cancer. I don't know how long she has left." Even as I spoke, the words burned like lava against my tongue. The thought of losing Aunt HoneyBea was bizarre. There was no way I'd be able to face the realization on my own. I needed Gia.

"Just go home," Gia said again before turning and walking away.

"What are you doing? Didn't you hear me? She's dying. Aunt HoneyBea is dying!" I hoarsely screamed as tears streamed down my face. I could hear my own words echoing inside my head as Gia continued to walk away. I wanted to fall to my knees, but D. ran behind me and swept me into his arms. I felt numb as he ushered me away from the building. My aunt was dying, our family was broken, and there was absolutely nothing that I could do about any of it. I felt powerless and defeated.

I can't remember much after the moment D grabbed me. The evening progressed like a blur. I woke up inside D.'s boat, but he was nowhere to be found. I walked out onto the boat's deck searching for him. It was windy on the deck. Small waves pushed against the boat, rocking it back and forth along the shore. As I peered over the edge of the boat, a horrid smell blew across my nose. It smelled like blood and intense musk. I turned and was frightened to see a very beat-up Old Man Pete.

"Oh my God, who did this to you?" I cried as he fell into my arms.

"Stay away from him, Rumor," Old Man Pete struggled to speak.

"Stay away from who?" I asked.

"D., he's dangerous. Stay away from him." My mouth gaped open with horror.

Rumor's Journal Entry 6

I can protect you from any attack,
With the swing of an iron bat.
I can rescue you from growing fire,
With hose water that shoots just a little higher.
There's nothing I will not fight,
To make everything alright,
But now I'm facing the biggest C,
An untouchable force destroying our family.
Disease has taken an axe to my family tree,
And down goes the root, our cherished Aunt HoneyBea.

CHAPTER 10

The Grimm Takedown
As Told By D

I love it when a plan comes together. I knew Harlot would recognize Rumor the moment she heard that ridiculous accent. Rumor was the perfect carrot for my rabbit trap. In a game of chess, the most important move is to find your queen. Harlot had an army of rejected girls; all just looking for somewhere to belong. With the queen in my grasp, I had control of the army that I needed to finally take down Nefarius and his goons for good.

My entire right side hit the floor with a loud thud as Harlot recklessly threw me to the ground. Harlot's girls all sat before us watching like a bunch of hungry wolves. I could tell that she had done some great work with brain-washing them all. They actually believed the female activist mumbo jumbo she was spewing. Not only did they believe it, but it was clear that at least half of them would die by it as well.

Their drive was exactly what I needed, and all I had to do was convince Harlot that our goals were the same. She wanted the black diamonds, and I wanted Nefarius dead so I could be with Rumor. It wasn't really that hard to make Harlot believe that Nefarius had the diamonds, especially after I realized that he was the bastard son of V. Gatto and Charlie Morello.

"It seems we have approached a crossroads. Our ranks have

been invaded by a man." Harlot spoke while digging her high heel into my ribs.

"I say we smoke that fool." Kanetra spoke with so much vigor that the right side of her face curled upwards with each word. She sat between the legs of another girl getting her hair braided.

"Hell yeah, smoke his ass," added another girl as they all became riled up with rage.

"Now ladies of course we can kill this sack of spit, but what good would that do? They would only send more. We have to cut this problem off at its source. This man was sent by another man, a wicked man. So what do you say ladies? Are we ready for war?" Harlot yelled.

As they all roared with excitement, Rumor's cousin Gia stood out like a sore thumb. It was obvious that she was lost in thought, no doubt concerning her conversation with Rumor. I intended to use this moment as not only an opportunity to get rid of Nefarius, but I was also going to get inside of Gia's head. She was important to Rumor; therefore I had to keep her safe as I mislead them all onto dangerous grounds.

As their meeting came to a close, Harlot kneeled down to whisper a warning in my ear, "I allowed your girlfriend to escape, but if you're lying about my diamonds, I will make sure she dies as slow and painful as possible." By the time she realized those diamonds were missing, Rumor and I would've already run off together. Nothing was going to come between me and my happiness ever again.

In the darkest hours of the night, the girls threw me into the back of a van. They were extra rough so as to not miss a single opportunity to inflict some extra pain. I was bound and separated from the van's seats by a thick, metal door.

"Gia, keep an eye on the grunt," Kanetra ordered.

"Why do I have to sit back here with him?" Gia complained.

166

"Look here, sweetness, I ain't totally sold on you just yet, so don't give me no talk back unless you want me to roll up on you one night and take a bite of that panty punani. Mmm, I bet you taste like skittles." Kanetra bit her bottom lip while tugging at a belt loop of Gia's pants. Gia cringed with disgust before quickly joining me in the back of the van. Kanetra slammed the door shut, and left the two of us alone for the long, dark ride.

"I hope I'm not imposing, but what in the hell convinced you to sign up for this mess? Most of these hoes don't even have a pot to piss in, but you have a cousin who broke into hell to find you. Why don't you just go home?" I stared at Gia making it nearly impossible for her to ignore me.

"Well you are imposing, so please mind your damn business!" Gia snapped.

"I guess I hit a soft spot, huh?" I laughed.

"How about I open that back door and accidentally drop you on your soft spot?" Gia threatened. It was cute to see her so feisty. I could see why the Boy Scout was so crazy about her.

"Calm down, ma. No need to get violent. I was just asking a question."

"Really? Well let me ask a question or two. Who are you and why in the hell would you bring my cousin to this place?" Gia targeted me with her revulsion like a set of finely sharpened daggers.

"She wanted to talk to you, and there ain't nothing that I won't do to keep Rumor happy. That girl is my heart."

"Get outta here. I know mugs like you. The only thing ya'll want outta women is wide legs and empty heads. Rumor ain't bringing either too the table, so what are you doing with my cousin?" Gia continued to interrogate me.

"You don't know a damn thing about me. I love your cousin."

"Well I ain't buying it. The word love is just a man's way of beating a woman into submission. I don't know what secret deal you have worked out with Head Mistress Harlot that convinced her to keep you around and let my cousin go, but if you hurt Rumor, I'll kill your black ass myself." This sounded like Gia's last warning for me as she turned away and ended our conversation.

Several minutes passed before we pulled up to gated grounds. Lights shined from the windows of the Johnson Family manor like a fluorescent lamp. The girls all stood eagerly waiting for their first taste of battle. That's when the pack of Rottweilers arrived to accept their challenge. The shame and anger of lying face first in a pile of crap while a pack of hungry dogs chased after me quickly returned to haunt me. I wanted Nefarius' blood and SHE MAN had become my one opportunity for vengeance.

"Ladies, tame the puppies," Harlot commanded. The girls pulled a set of rifles from the van and unloaded rounds of tranquilizing darts into the dogs. The darts must have contained strong doses because it wasn't long before the dogs were out cold.

"Kanetra, take Sasha and Carmen to the east wing. I want Ashley, Monique, and Lauren to cover the west wing. Kim, Dina, and I will break in through the basement. Are we all clear?" Harlot ordered.

"What about me?" Gia asked.

"Stay out here with the man. Depending on how this goes, you will receive the order to terminate." Harlot spoke to Gia, but her threatening eyes shot holes through me.

The girls all easily leapt across the gate and quietly dispersed throughout Johnson Manor. Gia was not happy about having to stay behind with me. She sat furiously pouting with both her arms folded across her chest. I could see the way they were ostracizing her from the group and the effect that it was beginning to have on her. She was primed for my manipulation.

"Let me get this straight, you left one life to free yourself of a reputation as a home-wrecking whore just to start another one as a lackey whore. Ay, I guess happily ever after is in the eye of the beholder," I said sarcastically.

"I'm nobody's lackey, so just shut the hell up!" Gia snapped.

"Really? Then prove it. You hate my guts. I represent everything that went wrong in your life, right? Kill me. Pull that trigger and do what you've been wanting to do since the moment you first saw me walking in with your baby cousin."

"Shut...up!" she screamed.

"Shut me up, Gia. Act on your own. Take some control over your life. Are you Hurley's whore, Harlot's whore, or Gia's woman? What's it gonna be?"

"Agghhhh!" Gia screamed. You could hear years of frustration exploding from her lungs. It was a scream so powerful that it left her panting for air. Her eyes filled with tears that refused to fall. Her hands trembled while slowly opening to reveal the lines of her palms. She threw her palms against her face and finally wiped the first tears away from her eyes.

"I don't know much about you, but I can tell that you're a strong woman. The immortal heart is not unstoppable because it can't be hurt; it's unstoppable because of its resiliency. Your family needs you."

"But what about SHE MAN? They'll come for me." she said.

"Look at me and believe me when I say, SHE MAN ends tonight. I promise you that," I said.

Gia knew better than to believe a word that came out of my mouth, but she also needed something to believe in. She needed some form of hope. I was her only option, so she untied the ropes that bound my hands. She looked me in the eyes while handing me her gun. Our eye contact made an agreement before she turned, leapt from the van, and raced off into the darkness.

Harlot left a digital two-way radio so that she could contact

Gia if necessary. I learned a long time ago how to activate the signals even when the other radio was set to silent. I could hear Harlot breathing as she sat against the basement door listening to the dinner party happening above.

"I'm sure you all are wondering why I've called you here today. As leaders of the church, I wanted to address each of you first. I want to talk about my plans for the future of Hurley." Nefarius's voice sounded through the speaker.

"Your future plans for Hurley? What's going on here?" Deacon Hamilton asked.

"I assumed Andrew Booker had informed you all that I'll be taking over as the new pastor for the Rock of the Delta First Missionary Baptist Church," said Nefarious.

"Deacon Booker, is this true?" Sister Mary Gibson asked.

"Mary, Deacon Booker and I both feel that Mr. Grimm's proven leadership can take not only the church, but this entire city to the next level," explained Sister Owen. Deacon Booker never said a word. Even through his silence, his regret could be felt loudly through the speakers.

"We are a committee. What gave you two the right to make that decision without the rest of us?" Deacon Hamilton asked.

"With all due respect Brother Hamilton, Andrew and I are the ones who have been sacrificing to keep this church afloat. We have been working our behinds off, and not even one of you can deny that," Sister Owen snapped.

"This is ridiculous, Deacon. You know this is wrong." Deacon Hamilton continued to protest.

"Let me assure you Brother Hamilton that I have nothing but the best intentions toward this church and this community. That is why I'm donating five million dollars of my own money to the restoration and expansion of the church." Nefarius said.

"Expansion?" Deacon Hamilton asked.

"He is funding his expansion with my diamonds. I'm going to bleed that bastard dry," Harlot whispered.

"Yes, expansion. We're going to take the church's outreach to another level. I want you all to think in terms of a mega-church. We're going to build satellite churches in key cities such as Atlanta, New Orleans, Birmingham, Nashville, and Jackson. Then we'll broadcast our Sunday morning services through cable television and broadcast radio," Nefarius explained.

"Television? Radio? I've always said that this face belongs on the big screen. I'm ready for my close-up, Mr. Grimm." Sister Mary Gibson, easily swayed by the prospect of fame, relinquished all of her doubts.

"Thank you, Sister Gibson. Anyone who is not for the expansion of this church, I will happily accept your resignation from the committee at this time. So are we all in?" Nefarius asked.

"It's time," Harlot whispered into the radio.

Almost in synch with her command, shots fired in the air. Glass shattered into tiny pieces as the ladies of SHE MAN invaded Johnson Manor. Like a tiny militia, their guns were blazing.

"We're in!" Kanetra shouted while shooting at Nefarius' men. Sister Gibson and Sister Owen's screams echoed through the radio's speakers.

"Cover me. Grimm is on the run!" Harlot commanded before bursting out of the basement and taking off in pursuit of Nefarius.

All-out war had commenced in Johnson Manor. Everything was going perfectly according to my plans. I pulled my cell phone from where it was hidden beneath in socks and called 9-1-1. I had timed everything down to the second. It would take the police exactly 15 minutes to reach Johnson Manor, so I had 10 minutes to ensure Nefarius's death. I grabbed the gun, jumped the gate, and ran for Johnson Manor.

I could still hear Harlot's heels as she ran off after Nefarius.

There was a loud bang as she kicked her way through a door. Her heart-beat pounded through the radio's speakers. Her steps slowed to a much slower pace. That's when I realized that she was in a standoff against Nefarius.

"Well, if it isn't Harlot Durst. My mother told me all about you; the desperate little girl who she played like a fiddle," said Nefarius.

"Let's skip the pleasantries, you overgrown hog. Where are the black cat diamonds?" Harlot asked.

"Now this is hilarious. You hear this mama? She's here for those damn diamonds." Nefarius chuckled.

"Who in the hell are you talking to?" Harlot asked.

"You're trying to tell me that you don't see her. How do you think I got the house or took my rightful place as the leader of the church? Mama's been with me the whole time. She played this city for decades, and now she's teaching me how to do the same," said Nefarius.

"You're insane. Your mother is dead. I killed her myself!" shouted Harlot.

"Yes, about that. Mama's not very happy about your betrayal. Mama wants you dead."

"Betrayal? That witch took everything from me and left me for dead. I risked it all to save her life. She betrayed me. Where are my diamonds?"

"Mama says forget you and your diamonds!" Nefarius yelled as gunshots blasted. I could hear them both crashing into furniture as they fought. Harlot grunted while struggling to fight off Nefarius's massive weight, but his creepy laugh continued to fill the background.

I rushed down into the basement through a long narrow corridor of steep steps. Spider webs clung to my face as I made my way into a large room stacked with boxes. As I made my way around a large book case, I stumbled into an electric Merry-Go-Round. That's when I spotted another set of stairs that led towards an illuminated doorway.

I scurried up the steps following the sounds of fighting, gunshots and screams. I stepped into a large dining room where fragments of a crystal chandelier were scattered all across the table. Deacon Booker lied in a corner with a gunshot wound to his shoulder. Sister Owen sat beside him weeping frantically. Deacon Hamilton and Sister Mary Gibson both lied on their stomachs weeping as well.

"You women make me sick. Look at you hanging onto the balls of these punk ass men. Well we ain't leaving here until all these bastards bleed dry." Kanetra walked back and forth across the dining room table with her guns raised in the air.

"Please just leave us alone." Sister Owen cried.

"I'll leave you alone, alright. How about I put another hole in that pecker-wood packing pussy of a man you're holding?" Kanetra laughed.

"Or how about you don't?" I stepped out of the basement with my gun pointed directly at Kanetra. She tried to shift her target in my direction, but she was too late. I pulled the trigger and my bullet landed directly in the center of her chest. She screamed and spit out a splatter of blood before falling backwards onto the table. The other girls sent rounds of bullets after me, but my diversion gave Nefarius's goons enough leeway to act. They attacked the girls. One of them was even able to snatch Kanetra's gun. I ducked into the hallways and took off searching for Nefarius as their gunfight continued.

As I approached the door to an office on the West Wing, everything was stone quiet. I slowly stepped into the room while keeping my eyes alert and ready for any sign of Nefarius. I turned the corner into the room and witnessed the destruction that had resulted from Nefarius and Harlot's fight. The office was a mess. I made my way towards the desk's chair, which was rotated backwards. I grabbed the back of the chair and turned it. Harlot sat both stiff and pale as blood dripped from the knife cut in her throat. I checked her pulse to find that she was dead.

"Nice of you to join the party," said Nefarius as I quickly turned to face him with my gun still loaded.

"This is the end of the line for you. I'm taking you down," I said.

"You're a smart man, D. That's why I hired you in the first place. I knew that you were the best, but I had no idea that you would be the one to reunite me with my mother. You see when I found out you were skipping out on the hustle that I hired you to play, I was pissed. I wanted blood. I trailed you to Hurley, and for the first time since I heard my mother was dead, she spoke to me. She's been speaking to me ever since I stepped foot within this city's limits. She told me that it was time for me to take claim of her empire."

Nefarius rambled on like a lunatic. His suit and face were covered with Harlot's blood. His eyes were both bucked as if he'd just seen a ghost. From listening to him, it was clear that he had been speaking to Gatto's ghost.

"I knew your ass was crazy, but I had no idea you were a real psycho," I said.

"No one is coming between me and my mama again!" Nefarius yelled before lunging at me. I pulled the trigger, but he was quick for such a fat man. The bullet only scraped against his suit after he managed to dodge its impact.

He almost broke my knuckles while squeezing the gun from my hand. I yelled as he lifted me into the air and slammed me through the office desk. Splinters of the broken desk pierced through my back. I felt as if I'd just been run over by a moving truck. I coughed up a little blood while struggling for air. As my blurred vision focused on Nefarius, his hands were raised and ready to beat me to death.

The only weapon that I could muster was my adrenaline rush. I ignored the pain and rolled backwards from the desk's remains. Nefarius sprang towards me once again, but this time, I grabbed a coat rack to block his attack. His fury filled blow broke the coat rack into two wooden sticks. I swung the sticks into circular motion and slapped with both halves. As he stumbled backwards, I charged him with a set of wild punches.

The punches did little to stop him. He grabbed my throat and started to strangle the life out of me. I struggled to free myself from his grip as he lifted me into the air. He did nothing but laugh at my attempts to free myself. Nefarius was too strong. I could feel the life draining from me. With all of his strength squeezing against my neck, I had no idea whether asphyxiation or a broken vertebrate would lead to my demise.

"Looks like the tables have turned, my friend. Your line ends here," Nefarius laughed.

I waited until he lifted me far enough into the air to kick my foot forward into his groin. It was a direct hit. I could feel his nuts crunching beneath my foot. Nefarius yelled like an angry baboon before dropping me to the ground. Even before I could fully catch my breath, I scrambled to locate the gun I had dropped. With the gun in my hands, I stood to my feet and pointed the gun directly at his head.

"Freeze!" Time was up. The sheriff's department had arrived.

"Thank you, God. Please don't let him kill me." Nefarius said while bursting into false tears.

"Shut the hell up!" I yelled.

"Put your hands into the air Mr. Ception. You are under arrest for the murder of Kesha Martin," Sheriff Mack said.

I looked into Nefarius' face and saw a slight smirk forming across it. How had he managed to turn me in to the cops? He had been a step ahead of me the entire time. "This man is telling lies. He killed that woman," I said while pointing to Harlot's dead body.

"They both attacked me, officers. I have a room full of witnesses. I was only defending myself," said Nefarius.

"We're taking you in D. We were given some pretty concrete evidence against you. Mr. Grimm had nothing do with it. You have the right to remain silent. Anything you say or do can and will be used against you in a court of law." Sheriff Mack proceeded to read my rights while throwing handcuffs around my wrists. I had no idea who knew my real identity to turn me into cops. None of it made any sense. I had everything figured out. My plan was fool proof, so how had it gone so wrong?

Sheriff Mack's deputies walked me out of the house. I dropped my head with defeat. Since the age of 14, I had been the South's most discrete hustler. No one had ever been able to figure me out; but for the first time, I was exposed. Everyone knew me to be the monster that I truly was. I could see them all shaking their heads with disgust. Their judgmental eyes dissected me into tiny pieces. I felt as if I was naked and bare-foot while walking against the wind on a street of hot coals.

I didn't imagine that it could get any worse from that moment. I thought I had hit rock bottom until I saw her face. Rumor stood before the police cruiser with eyes that were swollen from crying. There was no love in her angel eyes for me. She looked as if she was watching Satan himself.

"Don't believe anything that they tell you, baby. I'm going to get out of this. I promise!" I shouted with a final attempt at saving her perception of me.

"You lied to me. I opened up to you and you lied to me." There was so much anger in her words that it hurt me to even hear them.

"I meant everything that I said to you. None of this changes anything," I said.

"You killed your ex-girlfriend only a few weeks before making love to me. Excuse me, or should I say only weeks before smashing me. You almost killed Mr. Pete, and then you claimed his boat as your home. It was all a lie. Were you going to kill me next?" she screamed.

"No baby, you have to believe that I love you." My voice cracked in a way that I had never heard before. My face was warm, and my eyes were unusually wet. Something was seriously wrong with me.

"Love me? You violated me, you monster. You violated me." She cried before rushing me with a series of slaps against my face. The deputies pulled her away as she screamed all kinds of obscenities. Each word felt like a sharp blade against my heart.

As they sat me down into the back of the police vehicle, I felt lower than dirt. The sensations surging within me had left me exhausted. Something inside me was broken. It was a part of me that for a long time I didn't believe existed. My heart had been damaged by the same love that had given it life only weeks before. Who was I kidding? I should've known that happily ever-after's don't exist for people like me.

D's Journal Entry 4

How many demons have you seen redeemed from hell?
No grown man should ever believe in fairy tales.
I gave her a live heart but all she returned were broken
shells,
And now I'm the fool sitting in a jail cell.
No more life in me, my true colors are all pale
The man in me was killed by love from the second that he
fell,
So now I'm the beast of which the book foretells.

CHAPTER 11

Like Moses

As Told By Rumor

While lying on a bed of roses, sunlight soothed my skin. What I thought to be a warm breeze blew over every inch of my body. After a wide stretch and yawn, I opened my eyes to his perched lips. His Hershey colored skin glistened with the morning light. Our nude bodies pressed tightly together were arranged like the chocolate and fudge colors of an ice cream swirl. We were both connected by the velvet colored sheets that were wrapped around our waists. Our hips danced in a rhythmic circle as he planted soft kisses across the top of my breasts. I rubbed over every muscle cut of his broad back. His warm breath and kisses travelled up to my neck. My wide and innocent eyes met his tight and dangerous stare. The magnetic pull of his eroticism was too strong for any type of hesitation. I gripped his face before pulling his lips into mine. During the tender, wet moment in which our tongues collided, my body was filled with a brief but intense surge of what I can only describe as magic. I threw my head backwards with excitement before whispering his name. Then I took a Deep breath before rolling out of my sleep onto the empty half of my very cold and lonely bed.

It's frightening how even after witnessing the worst side of a person; we still have to deal with wrestling our hearts from their grasp. I couldn't stop thinking about D. I wanted to hate him for lying to me. There was a part of me that even wanted to kill him, but an even stronger part of me missed him. My skin ached for his touch. My ears throbbed with the desire to hear his voice. I hadn't even known him for long, but I couldn't even remember how to live without him. I lied in my bed all morning and used my sheets to shield my face from the sun. I didn't want to face the light. I found life to be a lot more comfortable while hiding in the dark.

"Oh my God, it's Darryl Junior!" Aunt HoneyBea's excited scream reached deep within my darkness.

"Come here, son. Say hello to your Aunt HoneyBea," Darryl Junior said to his son.

"He's so cute. Gia come look at Shawn. He's getting so big." Aunt HoneyBea gushed over Shawn, Darryl Junior's two-year-old son.

"Is that my big-head brother?" I heard Gia running from the basement as she leapt into Darryl Junior's arms.

"Hey everybody!" Chrisette beamed with enthusiasm.

"Now I know we didn't just take a road trip all the way from South Florida with a talkative two-year- old for me to come home to no Rumor. Where is that girl? She's the one who called us in the first place," said Darryl Junior. I pushed the sheets from over my head as I realized that I forgot to tell Darryl Junior not to mention Aunt HoneyBea's cancer.

"She's back there in that bed. That child hasn't left her room since last night," said Aunt HoneyBea. "I can't believe all of my family is together. I'm about to go into this kitchen and cook up a storm."

"Oh HoneyBea, you don't have to do that. With your condition, you should be resting," said Chrisette as I scrambled for my pajamas. I was tripping all over my bedroom while trying to stop them.

"Chile, what condition? Darryl Junior, what is this girl talkin' 'bout?" Aunt HoneyBea asked.

"C'mon auntie, Rumor told us about your cancer. Chrisette, Shawn, and I are here to help take care of you."

As I finally pulled my pajamas over my body, it was already too late. The bomb had been dropped and Aunt HoneyBea angrily screamed, "RUMOR!"

I fell into the hallway with an awkward smile on my face, "Welcome home."

"Now where do you get off spying on me and going through my things?" Aunt HoneyBea fussed.

"Auntie, she was worried about you," Darryl Junior said.

"We all are," Gia added.

"I worwy too," Shawn chimed in with his adorable baby talk.

"Well who can be mad at that cute little face?" Aunt HoneyBea softly pinched Shawn's chubby little cheeks. "I have stage three breast cancer. The doctors are confident that they can get rid of the tumor in my breast with aggressive chemotherapy."

"That's not too bad. You can beat that HoneyBea." Chrisette said.

"Yeah, but they can't do anything about the cancer that's spread to my liver. The damage is already too bad. I'm on the transplant list for a donor, but the chances of one becoming available anytime soon are slim to none," said Aunt HoneyBea.

"There's gotta be another way," I protested.

"Baby girl, all we can do is pray. But enough with all this sad talk, ain't no cancer gonna stop me from cookin' for my family." Aunt HoneyBea jumped to her feet and started pulling out pots and pans.

"Oh Lord, let me help her." Chrisette chuckled.

Aunt HoneyBea and Chrisette collaborated on a huge breakfast. Aunt Mildred rolled in on her hover round with a spoon and fork. We had hotcakes, grits, eggs, bacon, ham, hash browns, biscuits, figs, and fresh fruits. The kitchen smelled like a taste of heaven. I don't know where it all went, but we emptied every plate on the table. Even Shawn was able to find room in his little baby tummy for seconds. It was a family moment that I was sure Aunt HoneyBea would never forget.

In regular Hurley fashion, no good moment ever lasts long. Aunt HoneyBea stepped out of her bedroom with one of her best church hats on, "Everybody get dressed. We're going to church. Sister Emmagene says their supposed to be announcing the new pastor tonight."

There were only two days left until my birthday. My first love was a lying criminal doing time for murder, and on top of that, I was about to witness my father's church being handed down to yet another criminal. All I could think was happy birthday to me.

Everyone immediately began to prepare themselves for church service. I, on the other hand, was hesitant to witness Nefarius's ordination. Just as I was lagging behind everyone else and on my way to my bedroom, a familiar bark sounded from the front door. I turned to see Topaz standing on two legs with the other two firmly digging into our screen door. His tongue excitedly wagged from his mouth. I quickly dashed to my room to put on a jacket.

I stepped out of the door and kneeled down to embrace Topaz. I missed the sight of his beautiful blue eyes. He licked signs of his adoration all over my face. I brushed my cheeks and hands through his soft, plush fur as his nose sniffed through my jacket pockets. As I nearly erupted into a tickle fit from his nose poking against my side, Topaz pulled a small memory stick from my jacket pocket with his teeth.

"What's that?" I asked. He barked while dropping the memory stick into the palm of my hand. That's when I flashed back to the night before. I remembered attacking D. and slapping him continuously. I was so angry that I never even realized he had covertly dropped something into my jacket pocket.

"Auntie, I'll meet you all at church!" I yelled into the house before jumping on my bicycle and following Topaz out into the wooded area surrounding our home.

I sped off so quickly that I barely heard Aunt HoneyBea as she protested, "Girl, get back in this house." I couldn't listen to her. There was too much at stake. I needed to figure out what Topaz was trying to tell me.

Later that afternoon, almost the entire city of Hurley packed into the seats of the church. It was like Easter Sunday the way everyone showed up dressed in their best attire. I was very late as I arrived on my bicycle. I pulled up just in time to see Kayla sitting on the concrete steps that led to the door of the foyer. Her face was buried into her knees as she silently quivered.

"Kayla, shouldn't you be on the inside?" I asked while sitting beside her.

"I haven't been honest with you, Rumor. I haven't been honest with anyone." She pulled her face back to reveal streams of tears cascading down her face.

"It doesn't surprise me. I've learned that people lie. It's what we all do. What's wrong?"

"I didn't just move to Hurley with my family like I said. I came here alone looking for the man who is my father," Kayla admitted.

"Okay, girl. I'm not understanding. Just start from the beginning," I said while sitting down on the steps next to her.

"Girl, my mom, Kendra Evans, was born and raised in Hurley. She never used to talk about her past until the one day that I showed her an article about a little girl who took down a crime boss. She couldn't believe such a big story had gone down in her hometown. She went on and on about her friends who were mentioned in the article, like one of her best friends Alieza Arden." Kayla explained.

"Wow. Really?" I was stunned.

"Yeah, pretty cool huh? She also talked about my dad for the first time. She said he was a man by the name of Andrew Booker. She agreed to let me move down here and live with my Grandmother, Ms. Shirley Evans, for a year, so I could get to know him," Kayla continued.

"Wait. What? Deacon Booker doesn't have any children." I said.

"None that he knows of. He and my mom dated back in high school. After what happened to Alieza, she was afraid to give birth to me in Hurley. She went to NYU and has never returned to this city once since the day she left."

"Why haven't you told him?" I asked.

"I'm afraid. I can't just walk up to the man and say 'I'm your daughter.'"

"Deacon Booker's a good man. I spent my whole life not knowing about my dad. If I had the option, I would've wanted to know everything. At the very least, please give him that option." I said.

"Yeah, I guess you're right." She said while attempting to dry her eyes.

"Come on inside with me. It's about to be a pretty good show. Trust me; you don't want to miss a second of this," I said as we both walked up the steps to the church. I took a quick detour into the church's sound room. Lucky for me, Highlighter was working the sound system. His crush on me had amplified since I had become Hurley's most datable girl, and I used my new found clout to get him to play the recording on the memory stick. Not to mention the fact, that even in church, he was so high that I don't even think he realized what I was asking him to do.

"Church, are we ready to enter into the next phase of God's ordained leadership?" Deacon Hamilton's voice echoed through the speakers of the church. Usually Deacon Booker would have led the ceremony, but he sat on the front row with his gunshot injured arm in a sling. Kayla stared at him the entire time. "Then give a Holy Ghost hand of praise for our new leader, Reverend Nefarius Grimm."

Nefarius tugged at his suit jacket's lapel while soaking in the church's applause. His head was raised high as he looked down on those of us in the pews. All I could think about was how he had blackmailed Deacon Booker, and the way that his creepy laugh gave me chills.

After embracing Deacon Hamilton, Nefarius approached the microphone. As he opened his mouth to address the church, he was surprised to hear the recording played instead, "You're trying to tell me that you don't see her? How do you think I got the house or took my rightful place as the leader of the church? Mama's been with me the whole time. She played this city for decades, and now she's teaching me how to do the same." The audio repeatedly looped playing his words again and again as Nefarius' confident swagger dimmed to numbing shame.

Nefarius knocked the microphone from the podium and yelled all kinds of obscene words that were not appropriate for the church. The sound system squealed as a result of the overwhelming impact of his large arm against the microphone. His fuming eyes settled onto the sight of me as veins protruded from both his forehead and throat. The church burst into all sorts of flabbergasted chitter chatter.

"I'm sorry, mama, but I'm going to literally bleed this little city dry, starting with that stupid girl." The floor literally shook as Nefarius ran towards me. There was fire in his eyes. Just as he got within a couple feet from me, Topaz sped into the church and pounced on top of him. Nefarius cried out in pain as the large husky bit down into his arm. He stood to his feet and flung Topaz away. Topaz landed on his feet and barked several warning growls at Nefarius.

"This isn't over. You will regret this, Rumor Arden. Mark my words; Nefarius always has the last laugh!" he shouted.

"Get out of here." The people of the church yelled while throwing anything they could get their hands on at Nefarius. He shielded his face with his forearm while running out of the church.

The church was left in chaos as everyone attempted to process what had just happened. People were starting to get up from their seats. I looked up at Deacon Booker and Sheila Owen's faces. They had both sacrificed so much to save the church, but this may have been the final blow. There was no way the church would recover, and without the church, Hurley was doomed.

"Hitting rock bottom is one very painful fall...I should know. I've been to hell and back more times than I'd like to admit." Mickey grabbed the microphone from the ground and stood to face the church.

He looked amazing. I peered over a couple of pews at Sister Emmagene who smiled at me and winked. She promised me that she'd give him the best makeover, and she did an amazing job. There was actually a handsome face beneath the wild and bushy beard that had once covered his face. A pin striped suit flattered his body frame more than I could ever have imagined. By the way everyone stopped and turned to face Mickey, it was clear that Sister Emmagene had upgraded him to an eye catching level.

"My name is Markel Mickels, many of you know me as the dirty old man that sleeps on park benches with his dog. But what you don't know is that I was once the CEO of a fortune 500 company. I had a beautiful wife and an amazing son. To the outside world, I had it all, but I knew better. I was wallowing in unrighteous disobedience," said Mickey.

"Sir, we're going to have to ask you to take a seat," Deacon Hamilton interrupted.

"No, deacon, let the man speak," Deacon Booker said.

"Thank you, sir. In the book of Exodus, chapter 3 and verse 11 through 12, Moses said to God, 'I am nobody. How can I go to the king and bring the Israelites out of Egypt?' God then said, 'I will be with you, and when you bring the people out of Egypt, you will worship me on this mountain. That will be the proof that I have sent you.' You see church, God does not call on those who are qualified, God qualifies those whom He has called. When that calling comes, you will have all kinds of doubts. Moses had doubts. Think about it. This man was the prince of Egypt, but when God calls, none of that matters. In 1 Timothy 6:17, God said 'Charge them that are rich in this world, that they be not high-minded, nor trust in uncertain riches, but in the living God, who giveth us richly all things to enjoy.' Church, can I get an Amen?" Mickey's words translated into a powerful sermon, which was a fact made evident by everyone in the church returning to their seats.

"Amen!" the church shouted.

"You see church, like Moses, I was called from the top of the Forbes list to your local park bench. I lost it all: my wife, my riches, and my child. And Like Moses, I said 'God but I am nobody.' That church will not listen to some dirty old man that's sleeping on a park bench, but God said I have ordained you to free my people. Like Moses, you will lead them through the Red Sea of lies and deceptions and they will not be touched. Can I get an Amen? You will stand face-to-face with the pharaohs of this world that have left my people in bondage, and you will boldly reply, 'Let my people go.' "

I could feel the church pews trembling as the Holy Spirit moved through each and every person. My nerves shivered with excitement. I hadn't felt that much power in church since the last time I heard my father preach. It couldn't have been clearer that Mickey was standing in the midst of God's purpose for his life.

"Church, I am a living example that God's calling is not to be feared. Each of you has a destiny and a purpose. The fulfillment of that purpose is not to be measured by the means of man's riches. Your fulfillment will come when you have tapped into the lives of God's people. Stand to your feet right now and love your neighbor. Tell him or her that they are free from Pharaoh's chains. They are free to walk into the promise land of their lives." Mickey raised both his hands into the air before shouting, "Hallelujah! Gloraaay!"

The musical instruments played and the church both danced and shouted. During that sermon, there was so much healing in Hurley. Aunt HoneyBea cried and shouted with joy and fervor. Kayla both greeted and approached Deacon Booker to confess the truth that she was indeed his daughter. It all made me ponder on the events which had led us to that moment. Without D.'s recording, none of it would have been possible. Maybe God had called on D. He was certainly not qualified, but as Mickey proclaimed, God does not call on those who are qualified, he qualifies the ones that he calls. I had to speak to D. I needed to talk to him at least one last time.

I hopped on my bicycle and quickly pedaled towards the police station, but by the time I arrived, D.'s holding cell was already empty. One of Sheriff Mack's deputies was sporting a bloody nose, and the sheriff couldn't have been more furious. Before they could tell me anything, I already knew that D. had escaped.

"I promise you that we'll do everything we can to catch him, Rumor." Sheriff Mack said.

"What do you mean you can't help me? Somebody needs to find my son," Louise Vazquez's screams could be heard throughout the Sheriff's station.

"What is she talking about?" I whispered to the Sheriff. Ever since the day of my birthday party at school, Taylor had not been answering my phone calls. I quivered at the thought that something bad had happened to him.

"Apparently, she hasn't seen Taylor since last night. She says he left to take out the trash and has been missing ever since. We can't start an investigation until at least 24 hours has passed," Sheriff Mack explained.

I watched as Louise stormed out of the Sheriff's station with tears in her eyes. She collapsed to her knees before the front door. It broke my heart to see her sobbing so desperately.

As I pushed the door open to join Louise on the other side, it felt as if I were pushing a one ton weight. We had not spoken since she told me to stay away from Taylor. It was so hard for me to face what she was about to say. "Mrs. Vazquez, what happened to Taylor?"

At first she looked me up and down with a stone cold face. Her face then trembled for a while before it fully softened. "I'm so sorry, Rumor. You've always been there for my son. I was a fool to push you away. He was so distant from me after you left our house that day. I messed up, and now my son may be gone forever. I don't know what to do."

"Calm down, Mrs. Vazquez. You have nothing to be sorry for. You're just a mother who tried to protect her son, and there is nothing wrong with that. I'll find Taylor. I promise," I said.

"Thank you, Rumor. You know I always wanted a daughter, and I can't imagine ever meeting any woman more suitable for the job than you." Louise mustered a slight smile before hugging me tightly. She and I had never had a heart-to-heart conversation before. It felt good to connect with her on that level.

"Did Taylor say anything last night before he left?" I asked.

"Well now that you mention it, he had just found out about you finding Mr. Pete. I know he wanted to talk to you about it. Do you think that awful D. boy could have taken him?" she said.

"D. was too far away at Johnson Manor before Sheriff Mack arrested him. It couldn't have been him, but one other person is coming to mind." I said while thinking back to Nefarius's threats. He looked me in my eye and promised that I would regret exposing him. I was sure Nefarius had taken Taylor to get back at me. The only one who would be able to help me save him had just escaped jail. That's when I thought if I were D., where would I be?

While searching for D., I found myself once again facing the docks. Old Man Pete's boat had been removed, but D. sat on top of his motorcycle quietly facing the water. A large duffle bag was attached to the back of his bike.

"You shouldn't return to the scene of the crime. Isn't that the first thing they teach you in hustle school?" I said.

"It's not wise to track down the bad guy. Isn't that the first thing they teach you in good girl school?" said D.

"I need your help one last time. I think Nefarius kidnapped Taylor," I said.

"Let me get this straight, you want me to help you rescue the only other man you've ever loved?" D. asked.

"Taylor's my best friend. That's it."

"I believe that you actually believe that, but it doesn't matter. I'll do anything for those angel eyes. After that hell of a run I hear you gave him, I'm sure Nefarius is on his way back to New Orleans. Lucky for you, I'm on my way back there as well."

"Is there enough room on your bike for two?" I smiled.

"Nah, but there's enough room in my car for three. I'm coming too." Gia surprised me as she came walking toward the docks.

"Where did you come from?" I asked.

"Don't give me any trouble, Rumor. You're not going anywhere with this felon on your own. I don't trust him." Gia gave the exact same look that Aunt HoneyBea frequently used to let us know when she meant business, so I didn't dare argue.

Rumor's Journal Entry 7

When you've lost the right one,
They're sure to be missed.
That love hits a spot
That not anyone can kiss.
Daydreams and nightly steam,
'Cause you've never had it like this,
So close your eyes and leap for love,
It's worth your risk,
And what God has placed before you
Never let anyone dismiss.
If you've never seen your promised man,
Then how will you ever reminisce?

CHAPTER 12

The Big Easy
As Told By D

Inside of the Orleans Parish limits, I felt like a shark who had just returned to the water. Warm drops of the summer evening's humidity clung to my forehead like honey. It was the only place I'd ever been where you could smell horse manure, tobacco, fried chicken, and sweet olive all at once. The city was my domain. I thrived under the circumstances of the urban bustle. As we approached the French Quarter, it was packed with tourists. Many of them were there for the peaceful protests organized against the mishandlings of Nicholas Macon's homicide investigation, but the spirit of the city was still as live as ever. The smooth music of live jazz blasted from bars and nightclubs as alcohol flowed through the streets like rain water. Streetcars screeched across tracks while announcing themselves with a loud "wooka" noise that almost seemed like music to my ears.

I stood between street performers and statues of French architecture. I smirked at the sight of three kids fighting over a piping hot Beignet. As I took it all in, I was pleased to know that there truly is no place like home.

"Oh hell naw, was that a rat?" Gia complained while carefully walking along the city streets.

"Gia..." Rumor attempted to interrupt Gia's rude complaints.

"Don't Gia me. It stinks, it's crowded, and I'm ready to go home already," Gia complained.

"You could've stayed your ass in Hurley," I said.

"D., don't curse at my cousin," Rumor scolded me.

"You ain't gotta tell him nothing. After I finish calling the Po Po on that ass, he'll be lucky if he can take a shower without droppin' the soap," said Gia.

"Do you think I'm scared of Barney Fife and his squad of deputy dumbasses?" I gave her a look that made it clear that I was never scared.

"I wish the two of you would just stop. We're here to find Taylor, so can we just focus?" Rumor exploded. "D., you said that you knew a guy who could help. Where is he?"

"Chill out baby. Those angel eyes won't look so good with a bunch of stress lines. The place is right there across the street," I said pointing at Lestránge's Tavern.

Lestránge's Tavern was just like I remembered it. There was nothing quite like the smell of Neffie's prime cut steaks and hard liquor. The bar was lined with middle aged alcoholics and wild college students. They all eyed Rumor and Gia as if they were both items on the menu. Gia sneered in her normal conceited fashion, and Rumor tried her best to ignore the unwanted attention. I, on the other hand, shifted the handle of my revolver within my pants just enough to reflect the moon light into the perverts' lines of vision. Their heads quickly turned away from the girls as we continued to explore the restaurant.

In the back corner of an unlit section of the tavern, a man with unkempt blond hair covering his head and face swallowed his tenth glass of beer. Under the dim lights of the tavern, his hair appeared to be more of a dirty brown seeing as he probably hadn't washed it in weeks. If it weren't for the fact that he was wearing a torn leather jacket in the middle of the summer, I would never have recognized him. He wore that jacket as if it was his skin.

"I can't believe this is pretty boy Eric Troy that I'm looking at right now," I said while stepping into the stench of musk and booze. Rumor and Gia both quietly stood by my side as Eric scanned the sight of us.

"What the hell do you want, D?" Eric said.

"Don't get your panties in a bunch. I may be the last friend you have left in this town," I said.

"You don't have friends. You screw over everybody around you. If I were you two ladies, I'd run while you still can," said Eric while looking directly at Rumor.

"What is he talking about?" Rumor asked.

"Who knows? He already has a rap sheet longer than Aunt HoneyBea's grocery list. There is no telling what other ratchet things he's done," Gia retorted.

"Watch your mouth, Eric. We wouldn't want your secrets spilling into the streets. That couldn't be good for your father's upcoming promotion from police chief to commissioner. You know the one thing working class people hate just as much as a child killing cop is nepotism, and right now you're batting zero for two." I leaned forward to look closely into Eric's quivering blue eyes. I wanted him to sense my sincerity the same way that I could smell his fowl filth.

"Like I said, what do you want?" said Eric.

"I've got reason to believe Nefarius is looking to get into some human trafficking. I need to know where the next exchange is going down."

"You know I don't deal with Nefarius anymore," said Eric.

"You may not deal with Nefarius, but you've been off the force on unpaid suspension for months now. You can't tell me you're not still dealing."

"Man, keep your voice down. All I know is that there's a new cat going by the name of The Alchemist. He's been making a killing lately on the black market. He's hosting a ball in about an hour. If something is going down, that may be a good place to start," Eric informed.

"If this tip is a bunch of bull-dump, I will leak the information that you're the one who killed Nicholas Macon, so don't play with me, Eric," I warned.

"I promise its good info. Just remember that you didn't hear any of it from me," said Eric.

As I stood up to leave, Gia followed, but Rumor stayed behind and whispered to Eric, "I know you didn't kill Nicholas. Just stay strong, because God has a way of bringing truth to the light."

Eric didn't reply. He just looked into her angel eyes with a hopeful stare. I had no idea how Rumor knew anything about Eric's case. His name hadn't even been revealed to the press. On top of that Eric wasn't even sure if he killed Nicholas. Eric was the son of Police Chief Maxwell Troy. He joined the New Orleans police force out of pressure from his father, but Eric was a street thug like me. Even after he put on his badge, he used his police authority to control the streets. When he tried to blackmail Nefarius Grimm, he bit off more than he could chew. After being drugged at one of Nefarius's parties, Eric woke up one day covered in Nicholas Macon's blood. He didn't remember much from that night, but he never forgave me for taking the job with Nefarius to help instigate the negative public attention towards his trial. I didn't lose any sleep over it. Eric knew the rules of the hustle. A true hustler only has two friends: the first being his money and the second one is his gun.

"Rumor, you can't be getting all chummy with these people. You don't know what kind of hoodlums this criminal associates with," said Gia as Rumor caught up to us.

"Can I get you girls something to eat?" A large shadow grew over the three of us as we were approached by the owner of the tavern, Neffie herself.

"Not now Neffie. We're in a hurry." I turned around and faced Neffie's round face and double chin.

"I was talking to the ladies, chump. Besides, nothing's more pressing than a rumbling stomach." Neffie's raspy voice Deepened as she furiously eyed me. I was not in the mood to battle with the return of the planet of the apes, but Neffie was not intending to let us leave.

"Why don't you just mind your overweight business?" I asked her.

"Because a very special guest of mine wants to speak to you," said Neffie as I felt someone staring at me from behind.

I turned just in time to see five clenched knuckles soaring towards my face. The force of the blow sent me tumbling backwards. I could hear Rumor and Gia both gasping at the sight of my attacker.

"Yeah, I was waiting on you at the door," Ron Mack stood over me with his face just as tight as his fists. He smiled while looking down on me with his head tilted to the right.

I couldn't believe the Boy Scout had blindsided me. My head felt as if my brain had been run over by a bulldozer. Surprisingly, he packed some force behind that little punch.

"Ron, what is wrong with you?" Rumor asked.

"Why in the hell are the two of you with this con man? I saw the news about his arrest in Hurley. I ought to shoot him," said Ron. Gia was frozen solid. It was the most quiet I had seen her since we left Hurley. She was looking at Ron as if he was her favorite celebrity.

"He's helping us find Taylor," Rumor explained.

"You may want to calm down, Boy Scout. I'll let you get that one for free, but try that slick mess again and I'll bury you." I stood to my feet and faced off against Ron.

"I confided in you about the only girl that I've ever loved and you went to my hometown to run a scam on her family. You are the lowest low life I've ever met. What did he do to Taylor?" Ron said.

"The only girl you've ever loved," Gia blushed like a little school girl.

"Gia, please focus. He didn't do anything to Taylor. Nefarius Grimm kidnapped him. D. is helping us find Taylor." said Rumor.

"You don't need to explain anything to this pussy. I'll rip his head off," I said.

"Try it, punk!" said Ron. Gia held Ron as Rumor pulled me out of the tavern.

"I did my part and kept him here? Where is my money?" Neffie asked Taylor. I could no longer stand the stench of their company, so I stormed outside.

Outside the tavern, I stood facing the busy city streets. My nerves fiercely rivaled the action of the streets. Anger surged through me like electricity. I literally wanted to kill Ron. His threats sent me to a place within my memories that I hated to relive. Inside my head, I could hear my mother ripping the eight-year-old me apart with her words. The beast of me slowly brewed from within my turmoil.

"What is going on with you? You should see yourself. You're shaking. Your eyes are bloodshot red. You're scaring me," Rumor opened the tavern door to join me.

"Just go back inside with your cousin," I said.

"I'm out here trying to understand you. Just let me in. You've done nothing but lie to me since the moment I met you. When I look at you, everything in me tells me you're a monster and that I should stay away, but my heart won't stop loving you." Rumor said.

"What the hell do you want from me? I am a monster. I've killed people. I tried to kill that old man. I'm not the white knight in your fairy tale, Rumor. I'm the dragon."

"I don't believe you. You're not a monster. You're more of a coward than anything."

"A coward? Are you serious? Bring the Boy Scout out here and I'll show you a coward." I said.

"That's exactly why you are a coward. I've seen the real you, D. You're gentle and loving. You are not the monster that you want people to believe you are. You're a scared little boy who doesn't want to be abused by the world the same way that he was once abused by his mother. You created this monster to protect yourself, but it's not you. You don't have to hurt others to protect yourself. Your mother can't hurt you anymore. You're a grown man now."

Her angel eyes pried deep into my anguish. No one had ever figured me out so perfectly. There was no way I was going to admit it, but she was right. The beast in me was the only thing that had protected me from a childhood of neglect and abuse. I wanted to be normal, but I was afraid to face the world without the beast.

"You think you know so much about me. What about you Rumor? What are you scared of?" I asked.

"You already knew it from the moment you met me. I'm scared of dying as an unloved woman like my mother," she said looking away from me to face the street.

"What else?"

"What do you mean what else?" her eyes returned to me with a puzzled look.

"At first I couldn't figure out why you were wearing that black cat diamond around your neck. It just doesn't make sense to commemorate a woman who gave so much misery to you and your family, but now I get it," I said.

"She was strong. She was powerful, and she was so in control of everything. My father was exactly the opposite. He couldn't even control his own mind. Now after finding out Nefarius is actually my uncle, I see he's insane too. I'm scared that if I don't accept Gatto's mantle that I'll lose my mind like everyone else who came from her. I'm scared that I'm cursed," Rumor cried.

"You're not like them, Rumor. You don't have to be afraid." I tried to console her by taking her hands into my own.

"If that's the truth, then show me that I have nothing to be afraid of. Face your fears and I'll face mine." Rumor pulled her hands from me and walked back into the tavern.

My nerves were on edge as she walked away. I was afraid to let her down, but I was even more afraid of being vulnerable. I'd spent my entire life surviving and not living. Was it possible for me to let down my guard and face the world like any other man? In that moment, I didn't have the answers.

I walked back into the tavern shortly after Rumor. The Boy Scout had way more luck with his girl than I had with mine. Ron and Gia kissed passionately as Neffie stood before them gushing like a proud parent. I was disgusted, but Rumor seemed more than happy to see that Gia was pleased. I could see the tears streaming down her face as she watched the two of them.

"As much as I hate to interrupt this episode of the slut and the pedophile, are we still rescuing Lebron Lame or not?" I said as their annoyed expressions settled on me. Maybe I was afraid to be the good guy, but there was no denying how good I was at playing the bad one.

D's Journal Entry 5

My boogeyman didn't hide under my bed.
He wasn't the product of some childish dread.
My boogeyman was the head of my family,
She destroyed our home and snorted away all of our money.
My boogeyman was the danger in the streets,
He taught me to become what I feared I could never beat.
My boogeyman is the blood on my hands,
And the stains from my youth that I may never understand.

CHAPTER 13

The Alchemist's Ball
As Told By D

No sound is more overwhelming than the spirits of a man's past torment. Even when the knocking of my heartbeat echoes like a gong within my mind, the howling of my demons are the only sounds that I can hear. My nightmare was set in a messy one bedroom apartment on a building block of broken dreams. The electricity had not been paid in weeks. Nearly all of our furniture had been sold to support my mother's crack addiction. The cold air blew through our nearly empty apartment with such a vengeance that I could feel its freezing temperatures burning my skin.

My mother's cold and heartless stare dug into my soul like the devil's fingernails. She rocked back and forth to a beat that played only within her head. She may as well have been dead. There was no more human life left within her. The lease to her body had been transferred from her soul to the white powders of crack cocaine. She was a zombie; a shell of the woman that she once was. I could see her misery boiling from the tip of her tongue. A lashing was brewing, and as usual, I was going to be its victim.

"What the hell you lookin' at with your sorry ass? All you do is sit your black ass around here and eat up all the damn food. You're sucking me dry just like your damn rapist ass daddy." She spoke with such conviction as the words rolled from her lips with a touch of spit. I didn't say one word. I knew better than to engage her when she was lost within a drug high.

"You didn't know that, did you? That bastard raped me, and left his nasty ass seed here to suck me dry. I should've aborted your ass. You ain't worth the seconds that it took to make you. I took one damn look at that black ass tar baby that the doctor handed me. He slapped your ass to make you cry and I slapped you again to shut you the hell up." She threw her words at me like daggers. She kept shooting for the sorest spot, and waiting for the hit that would eventually destroy me. Tears streamed down my face, but I refused to utter one sound. I held it all inside as the pain burned like coals against my organs.

"I could've been somebody. I could've had my own life, but I lost everything trying to take care of your big head ass. Look at you. You're just as dumb as you look. I gave my whole life for a damn retard. I swear I should've aborted your dumb ass." Her eyes blackened with rage. Her voice elevated into a raspy scream. She leaned forward and yanked me to the ground by my ears. Torrents of pain tore through my skull as she bashed my head against the cold, hard apartment floors. I yelled for her to stop, but in our type of neighborhood, no one ever heard your screams.

"Take your retarded ass to hell where you belong. Die you sorry, bastard." Her screams grew louder. My head was wet with blood, but I refused to cry. All of my anguish continued to build within me until a monster was created. I was weak and defenseless, but the monster was invulnerable. It was stronger than anything I had ever felt. I blacked out. Moments later, I woke up to the same apartment, but there was blood everywhere. I was drenched from head to toe in hot human blood. My mother's body lied lifeless in front of me. Her face was nearly unrecognizable. Something had beaten her to death. From the looks of her appearance, any reasonable person would have determined that it was some sort of large animal. No man, let alone a small child, could have inflicted that kind of damage. But the beast within me was not a man; it was a ravenous monster that, on that day, received its first taste of human blood.

Looking down at the much larger hands of the man that I had become, I cringed at the thought of pain that my hands had caused. I wanted to weep for the woman that my mama had once been. I wanted to weep for the loss of her soul, but I couldn't. The monster had consumed me. I had hoped that Rumor could resurrect the man. At one point, it seemed as though she had, but the monster was once again regaining traction. I was too weak to defeat him. At 18 years old, I was still just as weak as that small, defenseless child.

"What's your angle, man?" Ron Mack sat watching me with hatred in his eyes. We were in Neffie's apartment which extended two floors above her tavern. The girls were both trying on evening gowns that Neffie had once worn many sizes ago.

"I got nothing for you," I said while looking at Neffie's bedroom door and wishing the girls would hurry up and relieve me of that moment with the Boy Scout.

"You're a con artist, right, D. or Darryl? Whatever the hell your real name is? I get that part, but what do you want with Rumor? Why did you go to Hurley in the first place?" Ron continued to question me.

"I'm here to help. Just be happy that we're on the same side for now because if not, I'd be draining the blood from your pathetic little body." My eyes cut into his direction like the blade of a machete.

"Are you boys about ready to lay witness to Neffie's work?" Neffie exuded energy as she burst from her bedroom door. You could tell that she was excited about the makeovers. I was excited to end my conversation with the Boy Scout.

"Yeah, let's see 'em," Ron said.

"Gia, honey, you betta werk!" Neffie snapped her fingers

as Gia pranced through the door like a true runway model. She eyed the Boy Scout with flirty eyes while bouncing and spinning through the living room. She wore a long, shiny, silver gown. It clung to her curves perfectly.

"Yaaasss, honey!" Neffie applauded with an exaggerated level of theatrics.

"Now prepare yourselves for the remarkable Miss Rumor," Neffie continued.

All time seemed to stop as Rumor emerged from the bedroom dressed in a black and silver gown. The dress's high slit revealed her sleek and sensual legs, while its plunging neckline accentuated her chocolate brown skin and high boosted cleavage. Just above her heaving cleavage, the black cat diamond shimmered for the world to see. She walked with less confidence than her cousin, but her coyness made her more appealing. Her braided hair was twisted upwards into an elegant up-do. Her beautiful face was artistically framed with gelled baby hairs. Our eyes locked as she flashed me a half smile. She was the most beautiful I had ever seen her. I wanted to rap my arms around her small waist, and pull her tightly into my embrace. I wanted to smell her sweet natural aroma. I wanted to feel every curve of her enticing body. I quickly looked away before my thoughts could arouse me beyond reason.

"I don't like to toot my own horn, but toot toot girls. You two are so hot that that ball may just turn into a full sized blimp!" Neffie laughed.

With the two hottest girls in the city by our sides, there was no way that we weren't getting into the ball. Rumor and Gia looked like Disney princesses as they stepped through the crowd of New Orleans' wealthy and elite. It seemed as if there were a line of women complimenting them on their looks, and an even longer line of men hoping for a dance. As much as they all wanted her, I was determined that Rumor was mine.

"Will you do me the honor of accompanying me for this dance?" I asked.

"Listen at you trying to be a gentleman." Rumor laughed.

"I'm serious," I said.

"D., this is not a date. We're here for Taylor, remember?" Rumor said.

"You're here for Taylor, but if you look over there next to the bar, you'll see a group of men. All of them trade on the black market. I've worked for some of them," I explained.

"Well why are we still standing here? Let's cut a rug," Rumor said while ushering me onto the dance floor and closer to the unsuspecting men.

With my left hand firmly planted against the lower dip of her back and our right hands together, Rumor and I twirled across the dance floor. We strategically circled around the wine table, careful to spy on the conversations of the gathering men. It was hard to listen from beneath the spell of Rumor's dance. The sensation of her body grinding against mine to the beat of the music nearly drove me insane, but even over the thrill of my surging hormones, my ears covertly listened to the discussion of three men.

A tall but skinny man with a tuxedo and a top hat said, "I hear Grimm is back. They say he's bargaining with one hell of a trade."

"That sucker's washed up. He should've stayed his ass in Hurley, Mississippi. It may be more suited to his new speed," said an older man wearing a checkered blue suit jacket.

"I don't know, Jimmy. I hear he's got him a number 1 requested draft pick for the European basketball association. They say the UK is looking to pay top dollar for the young man," said the third man.

"You hear that?" Rumor asked.

"Yeah, sounds like Nefarius is planning on selling your boy to some European black market basketball scouts."

"Is there anything they don't sale on the black market?" Rumor questioned.

"You'd be surprised. C'mon I think I know where it's all going down."

After learning of the type of trade that was happening, I immediately knew why the ball was being held in the convention center. Approximately every hour, from 6pm to 11pm, a large truck delivered what appeared to be food to the back of the convention center. But food was only a cover because the truck actually transported kidnapped people to the airport for international trafficking on private planes. There was only ten minutes left before the ten o' clock hour. We had to hurry if we were going to find Taylor.

Rumor stepped out of her high heels and followed me through the hallways of the convention center. Like Bonnie and Clyde, we were a couple on a mission. The hallways were long, and the building was large and complicated. My calf muscles ached under the pressure of so many steps, but my body was used to extreme situations. Rumor, on the other hand, could not handle the pain that flowed through her legs and feet. Her lungs thirsted for air. She stumbled to the ground, unable to take another step.

"I can't keep going. We only have a few minutes left. Please go find Taylor," Rumor begged.

"I ain't leaving you here," I said.

"I'll be okay. We're wasting time. Please do this for me," she plead.

"D. Ception, the Alchemist has been waiting for you." Two buff looking busters confronted us as we stood in the hallway.

"Tell him to wait in line with everyone else," I said.

"The Alchemist waits for no one," one of the men replied.

"Well, Angel Eyes, it looks like we've made these two jealous. I think they wanna dance." I was excited by the opportunity for a fight. The beast in me had been hungry ever since the Boy Scout blindsided me at Neffie's Tavern. I was past due for a good old-fashioned brawl to relieve some frustration.

"How about we place some fire beneath those feet?" one of the men said as they both withdrew guns.

"Damn, this is what's wrong with people. Nobody wants to throw hands anymore," I said as the barrels of both their guns exclusively targeted me.

"That's why you always bring a cop to a gun fight," Ron Mack walked into the hallway with his gun aimed at the men's backsides. Gia was by his side.

"We're trying to..." one of the men tried to speak, but I muffled him with a mouth full of my size fourteen shoe. Ron knocked the other one unconscious with his revolver.

"Rumor, are you okay?" Gia rushed to her cousin's side.

"I'm fine. Somebody's gotta go get Taylor," said Rumor.

"I got it, Angel Eyes," I said.

"I'm coming with you," Ron Mack added.

Gia remained behind with Rumor as Ron Mack and I dashed through the hallways of the convention center. After we were finally able to reach the back end of the convention center, unfortunately we were just in time to see the truck speeding off. Taylor was gone, but the parking lot wasn't exactly empty. Nefarius and one of his goons were preparing to board a brand new Escalade.

Nefarius sat in the back of the Escalade waiting for his driver to get into the vehicle. The smoke of his Cuban cigar covered the windows like frost. He smiled from ear-to-ear with a disgustingly satisfied smirk.

The door opened and Nefarius leaned backwards for comfort as his driver took the driver's seat. He'd had a long day. He was ready to rest for the duration of his trip home, but little did he know that his day was about to go very bad.

"Why aren't we moving?" Nefarius barked with frustration.

"Sorry boss, we got one more passenger to board," I turned to face Nefarius with Ron's revolver cocked. We had already left his driver laid out cold on the outside of the truck.

The back door opened and Ron climbed inside, "The Nefarius Grimm; I may even get a medal for this arrest."

"Mr. Ception, you are full of so many surprises. I'm sure at least one of those is a barrel load of horse dung." Nefarius laughed as if he hadn't just been captured.

"Speaking of surprises, you're going away for a very long time," Ron said.

"On what grounds, officer?" Nefarius asked.

"How about kidnapping and human trafficking just to name a couple off the top of my mind?" Ron said.

"Hmmmm... it seems we've reached a crossroad. This will be a huge arrest for you, officer; but what happens to you, Mr. Ception? Where do you go from here, besides prison? Do you think they're going to let you go? You're a murderer and a con man, the same as me. Rumor can never love you even if she wanted to," said Nefarius.

"Shut the hell up," I said.

"You know I'm right. You and I are the same. This young man is righteous. He'll never allow a murderer to walk away with his freedom. You have a choice to make. You can either be the villain who escapes to live another day or the hero who has to sacrifice everything and spend his life in captivity. Are you going to be the hero or the villain?" Nefarius continued to invade my mind.

As much as I had become aware of the mind games that he was playing, I couldn't deny the authenticity of his words. It was too late for me. I had already been exposed. Rumor could never love me. I had definitely come to a crossroad. I could feel my hand shaking around the gun as my fears culminated against me all at once. My mother knew that I would never amount to anything. I was a fool to believe that I ever had any other option besides being the monster that I am.

"D., don't listen to him. This is your chance for redemption man. You can do this." Ron tried to intervene but it was too late.

"You just made a fortune from selling Taylor to the Brits. Give me half the loot and you can have the Boy Scout," I said while shifting the gun's aim from Nefarius to Ron.

"What are you doing?" Ron shouted.

"You have a deal." Nefarius's creepy laugh hummed weird vibrations against the tips of my eardrums.

With a bag full of dollar bills in tote, I couldn't shake the feelings of regret that were running through me. Could it have been a sign of humanity or the disappointment that came with the realization that I could never be like other men? I had no soul. I was doomed to eternal damnation. Rumor deserved better.

I stood outside the large windows of the convention center to take one last look at the woman who had once loved me. She and Gia both stood over a body bag marked with the spray painted image of a golden coin. It was the symbol of the Alchemist. They carefully unzipped the bag to reveal its contents. I couldn't believe what I was seeing. It was Taylor. He seemed intoxicated by some sort of drug, but he also seemed healthy and within one piece.

Rumor burst into tears of happiness. She wrapped her arms around Taylor and hugged him firmly. I could sense her joy from the other side of the window. Her reaction confirmed my doubts. I would never have made her happier than she was in that moment. As much as I loved her, it was clear that she deserved better than me.

I turned to leave them to their celebrations. I was like the scorpion that had stung the frog after it carried him across the river. There was no redemption for me. The evil had always been within my nature.

D's Journal Entry 6

The man in me is now tired,
He can no longer cool his inner fire.
It's time to relent to a darker tide,
And grant the man his suicide.
Facing his tombstone, no one cried.
The same as when his childhood was denied,
There were no righteous men available to pry,
So grant this man his suicide.

CHAPTER 14

Time to Start a Riot
As Told By Rumor

Morning came and there was still no word from Ron or D. Gia and I were both worried sick. Taylor was still asleep from all of the sedatives his kidnappers had given him. I didn't sleep for one minute throughout the night. I sat beside Taylor's bed and prayed for God's help. It seemed like we kept losing at every turn. I just wanted the entire dilemma with Nefarius to end. I peered down at the black cat diamond which shimmered against my chest. It was a bitter reminder that my fight would never end. I was the girl who was responsible for taking down a crime boss, and on top of that, I was about to inherit her fortune. The criminal world would never stop pursuing me. The people I loved would never be safe. In that moment, I felt pretty low on choices.

"How is he?" Gia stood in the doorway to Neffie's guest bedroom looking at Taylor and me with a concerned expression.

"He tossed and turned all night, but I think he'll be fine. Any word from Ron?" I asked.

"Nothing. I hope they're okay. Rumor, I can't lose him again." Gia walked into the room with her head facing the ground. I could see that she felt just as overwhelmed as I did.

"I'm sorry, Gia. This is all my fault. I should've never let you all get involved," I said.

"It wasn't up to you. I wasn't about to leave you alone with that psycho." Gia pressed her hand against her hips and smiled with a slight amount of playful attitude.

"I know he's dangerous, but I still can't shake my feelings for him. Does that make me crazy?" I asked.

"Yes, but it's a normal kind of crazy. I've been there. We all have," Gia admitted.

Taylor rolled over in bed and started to groan. His face constricted as he tried to shake away whatever dreams were in his head. I took a fresh towel and wiped beads of sweat from his forehead. I hated seeing him so miserable.

"It's you, but I thought you were dead." Taylor whispered from within his sleep.

"Who is he talking about?" Gia asked.

"I don't know. He's been saying strange stuff like that all night. He's been through a lot. There's no telling what or who he's seen," I said while gently rubbing the towel against his forehead.

"You do know he's better for you, right?" Gia studied the way that I cared for Taylor. Her sight moved from me to him and then back again. She noticed the way that his body responded to my caressing him. She was impressed how even from within his nightmares, Taylor and I still managed to move in sync. There was a rhythm to our bond. It was a kind of rhythm that could only be found among best friends.

"Why does everyone keep saying that? We're just friends," I protested.

"You know what, cousin? When we were kids, they made us watch all these movies about princesses who sit and wait for the perfect prince to magically appear. We waited all our lives for that perfect man. We call him Mr. Right or our knight in shining armor. It's so ridiculous when you really think about it. There is no perfect prince. Never trust perfection. It's just a beautifully decorated form of deception. Trust what's in front of your eyes. Trust the path that God has laid out for you. He's right there in front of you. I mean what better man to devote the rest of your life to than your best friend."

Gia stood over me with her hands massaging my tense shoulders. I wasn't used to her speaking with so much wisdom. Life was pushing my cousin into becoming a seriously amazing woman. I couldn't even argue against her logic. I was just happy to hear her once again claiming God.

"I love you, Gia," I said.

"I love you too, Rumor. Now go take a shower. You're starting to stink. I'll watch Taylor," said Gia returning to her normal tough and rude demeanor.

I didn't want to leave Taylor's side, but Gia was right. The smell under my arms was like a bag of old onions. I followed the aroma of boiling gumbo down to Neffie's kitchen. Neffie was singing at the top of her lungs while stirring the pot to the rhythm of her song. Neffie's speaking voice sounded like that of a 60-year-old man who had been smoking cigarettes for half his life, but her singing voice was beautiful, smooth, and powerful. It was hard to believe that both voices came from the same woman.

Neffie turned to address me as I walked into the kitchen. "Morning honey."

"Good Morning. I was just looking for a fresh towel," I said.

"They're upstairs in the closet at the end of the hallway."

"I hope you girls like gumbo, 'cause I make the best batch in New Orleans," Neffie bragged.

"We love gumbo." I smiled, turning to face her living room television. The morning news blasted from the screen.

"They've been talking about that all morning. Somebody leaked the name of the cop who killed Nicholas. Nicholas' mom, Lawanda, is one of my best friends. I know all of this hoopla must

219

be killing her. I wish they would just let my girl grieve in peace," said Neffie as I stared at the television screen. Eric Troy's picture was plastered all over it.

"Why did they leak his name? I thought they weren't going to do that unless he was convicted." My voice cracked with worry.

"The city didn't leak it. Chile, you know cops protect cops. They say this leak came from an anonymous source," said Neffie.

"But they don't even know if he did it," I cried.

"Who else did it? Baby, somebody killed Nicholas, and that Eric Troy is just as corrupt as he wanna be. Don't worry yourself with all of this. Just go on upstairs and take your shower," said Neffie.

I couldn't tell her about what I knew. So many cops were killing black teens across the country, and people were understandably on edge. Eric Troy was however innocent, and I knew the truth. I couldn't allow an innocent man to be crucified for the sins of another.

Later as I showered, the warm water washed across my body. With the high pressured nozzle, it felt like an army of microscopic elves were walking up and down my back. I stood stiff as clouds of steam rose around me like the many thoughts that were soaring through my spirit. Visions of all the people I loved most danced around me. Then a giant black panther leapt through the steam visions causing them to dissipate into thin air. I stumbled backwards as the ferocious illusion pounced toward me. I closed my eyes because the panther seemed so real.

Suddenly behind my shut lids, I heard the bathroom window shatter. I opened my eyes to see a small burning flame growing outside the shower. The translucent image of fire was not an illusion, it was real. Embers twinkled behind the steam. Someone had thrown a brick rapped with burning cloth into the bathroom window. I pulled back the shower curtain, grabbed a wet towel and threw it over the flame. The small flame extinguished, but the screams from the other rooms in the house made it clear there were still others burning.

Covered with only a towel, I followed Gia's screams to Neffie's guest bedroom. Taylor was wide awake, but he stood on top of the bed swinging a broken lamp at Gia. I could hear the fright in his voice. He looked at Gia as if he had no idea who she was.

"Taylor, put the lamp down!" I screamed.

"Stay away from me. All of you just stay away from me!" Taylor yelled.

"Taylor, that's my cousin Gia. Don't hurt her! This is Rumor. I'm your best friend. I'm not going to let anything happen to you again. I promise." I steadied my voice to a more calm level and slowly moved to stand in between Taylor and Gia.

"Rumor?" Taylor's eyes finally rested onto me. "They're here. They're going to kill us."

"Nobody's going to kill anyone," I said while gently grabbing the lamp from his grasp. Taylor dropped to the bed in tears. I held his head against my chest as he sobbed like a baby.

"The sound of that glass breaking must have woken him up. What's going on out there?" Gia asked. Before I could even answer her, car alarms rang as more glass was broken outside. The whipping sound of growing flames taunted our ears. Shouts of protest and screams of terror all jumbled into one chaotic tune. Something was very wrong.

"Girls!" Neffie yelled from downstairs.

"Rumor, put on some clothes. We gotta go see what's going on?" Gia ordered.

I could feel my pulse racing throughout my entire body. My hands were trembling so badly I could barely lift the shirt over my head. Every time I tried to take a Deep breath to calm my nerves, I heard another crash, shatter, or scream. All hell had broken loose outside. The city's rage manifested through every corner of the streets.

As I tightened the last knot on my shoe strings, a car loudly screeched from beyond the walls. Whatever collision the skidding car had caused was so tremendous that I could feel the floors shaking beneath me. The lights flickered repeatedly before all together shutting off. Gia and Taylor had already gone downstairs to check on Neffie. I, however, was alone in the darkness. For a moment, everything was eerily quiet. The only sound I could hear was that of my increasing heart rate. I extended my hands out before me to feel my way around the room. That's when I heard the first floor board squeal.

"Gia, is that you?" I stuttered at the sight of a dark figure rising before the bedroom window. It was still too early outside for sunlight, but the little light that the night sky provided exposed the ominous figure. Even though I could not see his features, I could feel his eyes as they connected with mine. I opened my mouth to scream, but no sound left my lips. The terror of the moment had stunned my vocal chords into complete silence.

I turned and dashed out into the hallway. I fell but crawled my way back to my feet. I scraped my palms and knees on the floor. My legs ached as my denim jeans rubbed against the opened sore. I could feel him following me as he ran closely against my heels. I fumbled around the dark walls knocking paintings to the ground. The paintings hit the floor with a small thud, but it wasn't long before something larger fell. I turned to see that it was the man tumbling onto the floor, but before I could get away his hands gripped my ankle. My legs were pulled from beneath me and I quickly fell to the floor as well.

I tried to pull away but he was too strong. The man mounted me like an angry bear. I was pinned to the floor beneath his weight. He forced my arms to the ground. For some reason I was still unable to scream. I could feel his hot breath against my ear as he pressed against me. He stunk of fowl musk. I squeezed my eyes shut so tightly that I could feel tears gathering beneath my lids.

"I don't want to hurt you. You claim to know that I didn't kill Nicholas. If that's true, I need your help proving my innocence before it's too late." As he spoke, I soon realized that the man was Eric Troy.

If looks could kill, Eric Troy would be a dead man. Moments later Neffie's veins bulged with the tension she was using to hold back from strangling the life out of him. She looked at me as if I was insane for bringing him down to face her. Gia didn't hold back her detest either. Her arms were folded across her chest, and the muscle in her right cheek contracted with fury. We were all sitting before the bar in Neffie's tavern, except for Neffie who stood behind the bar maintaining a safe distance.

"You got some nerve bringing your child murdering ass into my home," Neffie charged.

"Yeah, what's wrong with cops nowadays? What's the need to kill black men all of a sudden?" Gia added.

"All of a sudden my ass! They've been killing black men since the day they stole us from Africa on those god-forsaken ships. The only difference between now and then is that they successfully brain washed us into thinking that racism died with Dr. King," Neffie explained.

"Why does everything have to come to racism with you people?" Eric rebutted.

"You people? I ought to open that door and let those rioters eat your ass up," Neffie continued. "My best friend is grieving the death of her only child, and your trash heart is still beating. What did that child do to you, Officer Troy? What did he do to anyone?"

Eric only shook his head in silence. I could tell that the weight of Neffie's lecture was weighing down on him, but it was probably nothing compared to what he had been through in the last few months. He was not the man whose picture was being blasted across the morning news. He was only a shell of his former self.

"Something wrong with your voice? Why so quiet now? You bigot cops usually have so much to say when you're on every block harassing some young black man. How many times have I seen you taking your frustrations out on one of these kids? How many times have I seen it? No one in their right mind will believe that you didn't kill Nicholas Macon?" Neffie scolded him.

"You're right. I don't even know if I killed that kid. I've done some messed up things to this community, but I didn't do them out of hatred for a color. I did them out of hatred for myself," admitted Eric.

"I was never good enough for my father, New Orleans's hero chief. He's the man who championed Hurricane Katrina and saved so many lives. How the hell was I supposed to fill those shoes? I'm not him. I hate who I am. I can't get anything right. I'm a habitual screw up, so I figured if I'm destined to be wrong then I may as well be good at it. For the first time in my life, I felt powerful bullying these streets with that badge. I was able to make this community just as miserable as I felt on the inside. It just so happens that I work a precinct which is majority black. Ms. Lestránge, I can't speak for anybody else. As for me though, I'm not a racist. I'm just hateful period." Eric confessed.

"Good for you, Officer Troy. Am I supposed to pity you? Am I supposed to give you some kind of trophy for admitting that you're an asshole? That child ain't coming back. Do you understand that? No mother should have to outlive her child. Because of you, Lawanda Macon has to live a lifetime without hers," said Neffie.

"Neffie stop. He didn't do it. Officer Troy didn't kill Nicholas Macon," I said.

"Rumor, how would you know that?" Gia asked.

"Because I know who did," I confessed as Neffie's face was left stunned with shock.

The awkward silence that followed was enough to make my teeth grind. Neffie's face was frozen into a dumbfound expression. She looked as though she'd seen a ghost. Gia tilted her forehead into her palm and paced back and forth across the tavern. Taylor was still quiet. He was even more absent of expression than he had been the day of my birthday party at the school. With that last thought, I realized that I had totally forgotten my birthday. In less than 24 hours, I was turning 16, and my day just kept getting worse.

Outside of the tavern, car engines revved loudly. Three cars came to a swift stop as several armed men stepped out. Eric's eyes swelled with an unnerving amount of terror. The three men aimed their rifles and blasted ammunition through the tavern windows.

"Not my tavern," Neffie screamed over spraying bullets.

Gia and Taylor both ducked beneath the bar. Eric took off in the direction of the back door. I don't know why, but for some reason, I ran off after him.

"Rumor," Taylor woke from his trance to try and run after me, but Neffie caught hold of his shirt. She held him down as bullets continued to fly over the bar.

The back door of Neffie's tavern led Eric and I down a very thin alley. We could hear the footsteps of the men as they pursued us. Luckily, Eric's car was not far from the back alley. He jumped into the passenger seat and handed me his keys.

"Why are you giving me your keys? They're behind us!" I screamed.

"That's exactly why I need you to drive. I can't be seen in this city right now. I'm going to lay low in the backseat. Please drive," said Eric.

"I don't know how to drive." My hands shook as I stuck the keys into the ignition. A bullet shot through the passenger side window and soared over my head. I screamed while pushing the pedal to the floor.

I hit about three parked cars while wildly jerking the wheel of Eric's car. I panicked and screamed as bullets sparked from all around me. My foot was still flat against the accelerator. The wheels of Eric's car spun quickly beneath the pressure of my heavy foot. We were heading full speed toward an impact with a small corner store.

"Ease off the gas and straighten your wheel towards the street!" Eric yelled while peering from behind the two front seats.

I did as he directed. As I turned the wheel, the side of his car swept against the brick wall of the corner store, but fortunately we didn't hit it. My hands trembled as I tried my best to keep the wheel steady. The streets and morning sky both blurred into one giant abstract scene as we continued to speed down the road.

"You're doing well, Rumor." Eric tried to comfort me. He could tell that I was beyond mortified.

Within minutes, we had cleared the French quarter. My nerves steadily calmed as the armed men were no longer pursuing us. Eric remained low in the car's back seat. All I could think about was Gia and Taylor. I was praying that we'd lured the gunmen away from them. If anything happened to either of them, I would never be able to forgive myself.

"Where are we heading because eventually we're going to run out of gas?" I asked as we randomly drove in no particular direction.

"You keep telling me that you know I'm innocent. How can we prove it?" Eric said.

"We should probably start with the man who framed you," I said. "Nefarius."

By the way his mood quickly turned sour, I could tell that Eric already knew exactly who was responsible for his problems.

God was clearly listening to our conversation; because the

music on the radio was suddenly interrupted by breaking news, "Recent reports are that rioters have raided the New Orleans Municipal Court with military grade weaponry. They have several hostages including judges, defense attorneys, prosecutors, and the officer behind Chief Troy's now defunct police community relations initiative, Ronald Mack. Police have been told that if former officer Eric Troy is not turned over to rioters before noon today, hostages will be killed. This has been breaking news. Stay tuned as we will continue to provide updates every hour."

"It looks like Nefarius finally got the war he's been searching for," said Eric.

"We can't let them kill Ron," I said, eyeing Eric through the rear-view mirror.

"We're not going to. Make this left. We're going to the courthouse."

The closer we came to the courthouse, the louder the police sirens rang. We watched as angry rioters effortlessly set fire to government buildings. Billows of dark smoke consumed the air. Flames roared from the tops of buildings like wild animals. By the looks of the sky, it did not look like morning at all. I squinted as the remnants of pepper spray flowed through the car's vents. Spicy tear drops flowed from my eyes. Citizens screamed and cried as officers brutally rushed them with batons. Police officers were on edge as reports of civilian sharp shooters came through. The city had become a real live war zone.

I continued to carefully drive until we reached a barricade set up by New Orleans finest. I turned to Eric and whispered, "How are we going to get through? The cops have this entire section of the city blocked off."

"We're not going to go through," he said.

"What do you mean? Why not?" my voice raised a few decibels as I tried to understand why he changed his mind.

"I've gotta do this on my own. Thanks for your help with getting me this far, but I can't put your life in anymore danger."

"They have Ron. I gotta help," I said.

"No, you have to finish your childhood. Go home and hang with your friends or something. I appreciate you helping me with this, I really do. But this is too heavy for a girl your age. You've seen how chaotic it is in there." Eric didn't even give me a chance to argue. He quickly jumped out of the car and revealed himself to the other officers. They both seized him as if he was a wanted fugitive. The breath of my screams left fog on the passenger seat window as they struck his head with their guns. Eric fell unconscious. As he solemnly slept, the source of all our nightmares stepped out of the police cruiser. It was Nefarius Grimm.

"Let him go," I screamed while falling out of Eric's car.

"I'm glad that you could join us, Rumor. You and I have a score to settle." Nefarius grinned.

"You're supposed to be police. That man is a criminal. Arrest him!" I shouted.

"They work for me. Grab the little wench too," Nefarius ordered as the two officers grabbed me and threw me into the back of the police cruiser along with Eric.

I was forcefully escorted through the courthouse past a horde of scorned men with guns. There was so much hatred in their eyes, and they had already beaten Eric bloody on the way to the courthouse. I'd never been more afraid in my life. They threw us both into a courtroom where Nefarius sat on the judge's bench. Ron was already there. They had him handcuffed to the defendant's seat. They dragged Eric further out onto the floor where he lied submissively before Nefarius. He was much too damaged to even think of escaping.

"Welcome to my world, Rumor. The irony of this situation is that this is a court of law; the place where justice should be held supreme. In recent years, America has lost this founding Principal of justice. But today, in this government building, we are establishing a new set of principles." Nefarius stood above the court as if he were some sort of king on a throne.

"What do you think is going to happen here? You have hostages in a courthouse. You're not getting out of this situation with your freedom. It's only a matter of time before the National Guard gets here." I approached the bench to face off against Nefarius's wicked scowl.

"I welcome them as well. This is only the beginning. You see although Mr. Troy's case may be phony, there are so many others across this country that aren't. This case is just the necessary catalyst. Once the media shows black America our success in executing Officer Troy, the rest of the country will galvanize behind our cause. I'll provide them with their weaponry and leadership. Before you know it, I'll be the wealthy and powerful man that I was always destined to be. Mother will be so proud."

"You are crazy as hell," I said.

"Let her go, Nefarius. This is between you and me. You don't need her." Eric grunted through his pain.

"I don't think so Troy. I want Rumor to see this." Nefarius laughed as a group of rioters entered the court room. They were all armed. I immediately knew what was about to happen.

"Please don't do this. You all have to believe me. Eric Troy did not kill Nicholas Macon," I cried while standing between Eric and the rioters.

"Rumor, get away from there!" Ron yelled while yanking at his handcuffs.

"No, she can stay there. We know Eric Troy didn't kill Nick," one of the rioters said.

"What are you fools talking about? We have to ensure justice for Nicholas Macon. Kill Officer Troy now!" Nefarius ordered, but the rioters did not budge.

"Andrew Booker just confessed to everything on national news. You're behind all of this, Nefarius. You tried to play this city for the last time!" Another rioter shouted. Deacon Booker had finally come through with the truth. I knew that there was no way he'd let me down.

"I don't believe this. I guess if you want something done right, you have to do it yourself." Nefarius stood to his feet and pulled a gun from beneath his suit jacket. He quickly cocked the gun and aimed the barrel at my head.

"Nefarius, put down the gun!" a rioter shouted. Some of them aimed their guns at Nefarius, but the others were focused on Nefarius's goons who, by then, set targets on the rioters.

"Not before I kill little Miss Rumor. You ruined everything for me and my mother. Mother wants this. Mother wants me to take your life!" Nefarius shouted.

"We'll shoot you, Nefarius!" the rioter warned again.

"I'm sure you will, but not before I shoot her."

"Go ahead. Shoot me!" I screamed. "It's not going to stop your pain, Nefarius. She abandoned you. She pretended like you didn't even exist while she played preacher's wife with another son. I'm not the one who hurt you. She did!"

"Don't you dare lie on my mother, she loved me. Your father took her away from me!" Nefarius barked with fury as his finger teased the gun's trigger.

I closed my eyes and prepared to die. I wanted to see my mother. I could hear her singing in my head. The beauty of her voice nearly muted the sound of the gun as the bullet finally fired.

I opened my eyes expecting to see the pearly gates. I imagined that Alieza would be there waiting for me. I imagined that her smile would brighten even the heavens. She extended her hands and welcomed me to eternal paradise, but that was not what I saw at all. I opened my eyes to a pale Nefarius. His eyes rolled into the back of his head until only the whites were showing. There was a bullet sized hole in the middle of his forehead. He fell backwards into the judge's seat where he took his final breath.

I turned around to see where the bullet had come from, and D. stood out from the protestors with a smoking pistol in his hand. The doors to the courtroom burst open as troops of National Guardsmen invaded the room. They tackled the group of protestors and Nefarius's men to the ground. Unfortunately D. was also taken as an accomplice to the madness. As he lied with his stomach to the floor and his hands cuffed behind his back, D. never stopped looking at me. His eyes were not full of sorrow or regret, they were full of love. He had made a choice. He sacrificed everything, even the monster that he had become so dependent upon, to save me. As our eyes connected, I could see that the man I loved had successfully redeemed his soul. My eyes were no longer the only windows to the soul of an angel. D.'s soul was touched by God as well. It was an unbelievably beautiful moment.

As the National Guardsmen pulled him to his feet by his handcuffed arms, he mouthed the words, "I love you." I stood to my feet, ran to him, and planted the most passionate kiss that I could manage on his lips. The officers tried to pull me away, but D. and I were like magnets the way we attracted one another.

When I finally released him from my grip, I screamed, "I love you too!" He only nodded and smirked as they pulled him further away. He couldn't open his mouth to reply because I left him a small gift. Through our kiss, I had given him my symbol of strength. On the tip of his tongue, D. secretly held the black cat diamond.

Outside of the courthouse, Aunt HoneyBea stood with both Gia and Taylor by her side. They were all waiting for me. Aunt HoneyBea's eyes were full of tears. She hugged me with her signature embrace. All I could do was weep on her bosom. Nefarius was finally gone. My nightmare was finally over. It was indeed a happy birthday for me.

Rumor's Journal Entry 8

What kind of story would it be,
if we never had to pass the test of time?
What sort of ending would we see,
if we never had any hurdles to climb?
As I take our struggles in stride,
with true love drifted the strongest tide.
It's been one helluva ride,
and my love, you and I,
we have a romance to write.

CHAPTER 15

If The Truth's Gonna Hurt
As Told By Rumor

I have a confession to make. Many years ago, the most important woman in my life explained to me, "... if the truth is gonna hurt then I gotta tell a lie." Well I may have omitted certain parts of my story mostly because of a lingering fear that it was all a delusion. Some events were so surreal that they could've been easily misconstrued for dreams. In order to spare myself of any further pain, I chose to ignore the obscurest moments of my reality.

Let me start by going as far back as the day of my mother's death. I looked into what appeared to be her lifeless eyes pressed against a shattered and bloody windshield, but what I cannot erase from my mind is the second in which her eyes blinked. The coroner told us that she was dead, but no family member was needed to view her body. The funeral was closed casket because apparently the damage to her cranium was too severe for her body to be prepared for viewing. As a result, none of us ever saw her again.

Now I'll fast forward to the afternoon that Nefarius was supposed to be ordained as the new head minister of the church. Before I arrived to church, I followed Topaz to the field of butterflies. I had no idea where we were going, but I could feel in my gut that something important was about to happen. Butterfly wings flickered across the edges of flowers. They seemed to dance around us as we pushed through the high grass. After what felt like several miles of bike riding, we came to a stop on the other side of the field. Taylor and I rarely ever went that far into the field. I had forgotten all about the marsh that was there.

Standing before the edge of the marsh was Mickey and a woman who was cloaked with a black veil. I could almost see her eyes through the veil. They were so familiar that I would have rather denied my eyes the sight of them. They looked exactly like my mother's, but I knew that was impossible so I ignored my instincts.

"Rumor, I have someone I'd like you to meet," said Mickey, pointing towards the veiled woman.

"What's going on here?" I asked.

The woman did not speak. She only handed me an envelope which was marked with a seal designed in the shape of a golden coin. The words, "Pursue the treasures of life," were inscribed around the edges of the seal. My eyes watered as torrents of emotion built up inside of me. That's when I realized that the veiled woman had to have been my mother. She was some sort of ghost or phantom. I knew that no one would ever believe me. I had to see the face that was behind the veil. Before I could look up from the envelope, the woman had already disappeared into the high grass and flowers of the field.

"Was that my mama?" I asked Mickey. The confusion was too much. My hands quivered uncontrollably.

"All will be revealed in God's time. Don't open the letter until He gives you a sign," Mickey answered.

"I'm so confused, Mickey. I don't know what to do anymore. I don't even know if I can trust the things that I'm seeing. I'm losing my mind just like my dad, but at the worst time possible. My aunt is very sick and my family needs me," I cried.

"Pray with me, Rumor." Mickey took my trembling hands into his own. There was so much anointing in his touch. I could feel the calming presence of his spirit as my hands were instantly eased.

"Father in the name of Jesus, I pray that You pour into the life of this young woman the order of your perfect plan. She has a light, Father God, which has led so many across this nation into Your will. Father You said in 2 Chronicles 7:4 that "if Your people, who are called by Your name, will humble themselves and pray and seek Your face and turn from their wicked ways, that You will hear from heaven and forgive their sins." Father this child has stood firm in the face of evil and purged Your temple of its wicked ways. She is a warrior for Your will. I pray that the bondage of generational curses is broken from this child's mind. In your son, Jesus's name, she will be made whole. We love You Father and we thank You for Your many blessings. This and all things we pray in the name of your son, Jesus Christ. Amen."

"Amen," I opened my eyes to so much more clarity. Mickey was without a doubt a shepherd for God's people. The Rock of the Delta First Missionary Baptist Church needed a true shepherd because our city was once again falling apart. I put my own desires aside and tucked the envelope into my back pocket. I had to get Mickey ready for church, and I was running very short on time.

I convinced myself that the woman was only a figment of my imagination. She didn't cross my mind again until the second time I saw the symbol of the golden coin. It was on the body bag the night that Gia and I found Taylor. It belonged to the Alchemist; a name which was also the title of my mother's favorite book. It was a sign from God, the sign Mickey had instructed me to wait for.

Between worrying about Taylor, the riots, and Nefarius, I still didn't get a chance to open the envelope until the morning of my 16th birthday. I stood facing 16 candles with all of my family and friends surrounding me. Tami was as crazy as ever. She brought along some tall, dark, and dubious looking brother. With her new flavor of the week in the house, we had to keep an eye on all the valuables. When it comes to Tami some things never change, but I wouldn't trade her for the world. I couldn't believe that there was ever a time that we didn't like each other, because I loved her like a sister. The Bookers came through to show their love. Deacon Booker was free on bond while waiting for his trial to begin in the Nicholas Macon case. His new wife, Sheila Booker, and his new-found daughter, Kayla, both stood by his side as the family that he'd always wanted.

Ron Mack was also there. He moved back to Hurley where his father accepted him with open arms. He and Gia held hands while proudly displaying their love to the world. Darryl Junior, Chrisette, and Shawn also embraced one another. I couldn't help but notice the small bump forming in Chrisette's stomach. I was sure they were expecting another addition to their family. Sister Emmagene finally found her a good man. She and Mickey had not only seen the beauty inside of one another, but as a couple they were able to bring it to the surface. She made him a better man, and he directed her on a path to becoming a better woman.

Louise couldn't stop hugging Taylor. She was so happy to have him back home where he belonged. Throughout that morning, she didn't miss one chance to remind me of how grateful she was that I was Taylor's best friend. As for Taylor and I, we were soul mates. He would always be a fixture in my life, but he decided to work things out with Rima to give their child a chance at having a family. I gave them my full support, and surprisingly Rima showed up to help me celebrate my birthday.

Aunt HoneyBea pushed Aunt Mildred in her old wheelchair to a place at the table as everyone waited for me to blow out the candles. You couldn't tell that she was facing a long, hard battle with cancer from the firm and assured look on her face. My aunt was a strong woman. There was not one doubt in my mind that she wouldn't be able to beat the disease.

I stood from the table and observed them all, "I already got my wish. I can't ask for anything else. My heart is so full of happiness right now. I love each and every one of you, so is it okay if we all share this wish?"

"It's your party baby. We can do whatever you want." Aunt HoneyBea provided a confirming smile. Everyone blew into the candles, and the smoke of all our dreams flowed towards the heavens.

A year had passed since my 16th birthday, and Hurley, Mississippi was no longer my home. I'm guessing that you all are still wondering what was in the sealed envelope. Well when I finally opened that envelope, I found a one way ticket to Paris, France. Because of the money that I inherited, I was already officially a millionaire. The opportunities were endless. Just as the words inscribed around the seal had read, I needed to pursue my personal treasure.

To this day, I still live in Paris. I feel so free in a world where no one knows the little girl who defeated the crime boss. Mickey preached about how he'd given up his fortune to pursue his personal treasure, but he never told us what he had done with his millions. Well apparently, he met a young woman who was beaten down and nearly killed by life, but her faith remained strong. She allowed the world to think she was dead out of hope that the criminal world would not retaliate against her daughter. Mickey was touched by her story. Influenced by God's will over his life, he provided her the means to safely spend her life with her only child.

"I never get tired of looking at the Eiffel Tower. It's so beautiful." I stood facing the city's greatest structure as the winds of France blew through my natural hair, which by then had grown down my back.

"I never get tired of looking at you," said my mother. Her face was like a classic painting from within my mind. I had spent so many years studying the beauty of her being that I still couldn't believe that she actually existed.

I took her hand into my own and inhaled the sweet air of freedom. I'd gone through so much while desiring the love of a man, but nothing in this world could ever trump the true love of a mother. Next time you're closing your eyes and wishing on a set of candles, remember to dream as big as possible because impossibility is sort of like perfection. Neither of them are concepts that actually exist in real life.

ABOUT THE AUTHOR

J.E. Tyler is an author, poet, and entrepreneur determined to find success as a published fiction author. It is the realization of this dream that motivated Tyler to found his publishing company, Zodiac Gifted Publishing also known as ZOGI Media and Publishing. Through this imprint, Tyler has self-published the dramatic science fiction novel **REG Aftermath** and the spiritually inspiring and dramatic novel **Rumor: Daughter of Lies**. Tyler has written stage play productions for his hometown church, Destiny Vision Christian Center. He is also the author of the well-reviewed short stories, **The Girl Who Stole from Fire** and **That Dance That We Do**. Tyler obtained a Bachelor's of Science in Business Management from Alabama A and M University, where he crossed the burning sands of Alpha Phi Alpha Fraternity, Incorporated. He also has a Master's of Business Administration from Texas A and M University. Look for this young man to utilize his God given talents and well-educated business acumen to dominate the book publishing industry and more in the future.

Please feel free to email Tyler at jtyler1985@live.com with any questions regarding his past, current, or upcoming novels. Your feedback is greatly appreciated.

Made in the USA
Las Vegas, NV
22 March 2022

46112796R00142